Till We Have Built Jerusalem

The Bloody Western Frontier in the Civil War Era

Alan E. Craven

MILFORD HOUSE

Milford House Press
Mechanicsburg, Pennsylvania

MILFORD HOUSE

an imprint of Sunbury Press, Inc.
Mechanicsburg, PA USA

For information about special discounts for bulk purchases, please contact Sunbury Press Orders Dept. at (855) 338-8359 or orders@sunburypress.com.

To request one of our authors for speaking engagements or book signings, please contact Sunbury Press Publicity Dept. at publicity@sunburypress.com.

ISBN: 978-1-62006-186-2 (Trade paperback)

Library of Congress Control Number: 2019939521

FIRST MILFORD HOUSE PRESS EDITION: April 2019

0 1 1 2 3 5 8 13 21 34 55

Set in Bookman Old Style
Designed by Chris Fenwick
Cover by Lawrence Knorr
Edited by Chris Fenwick

Continue the Enlightenment!

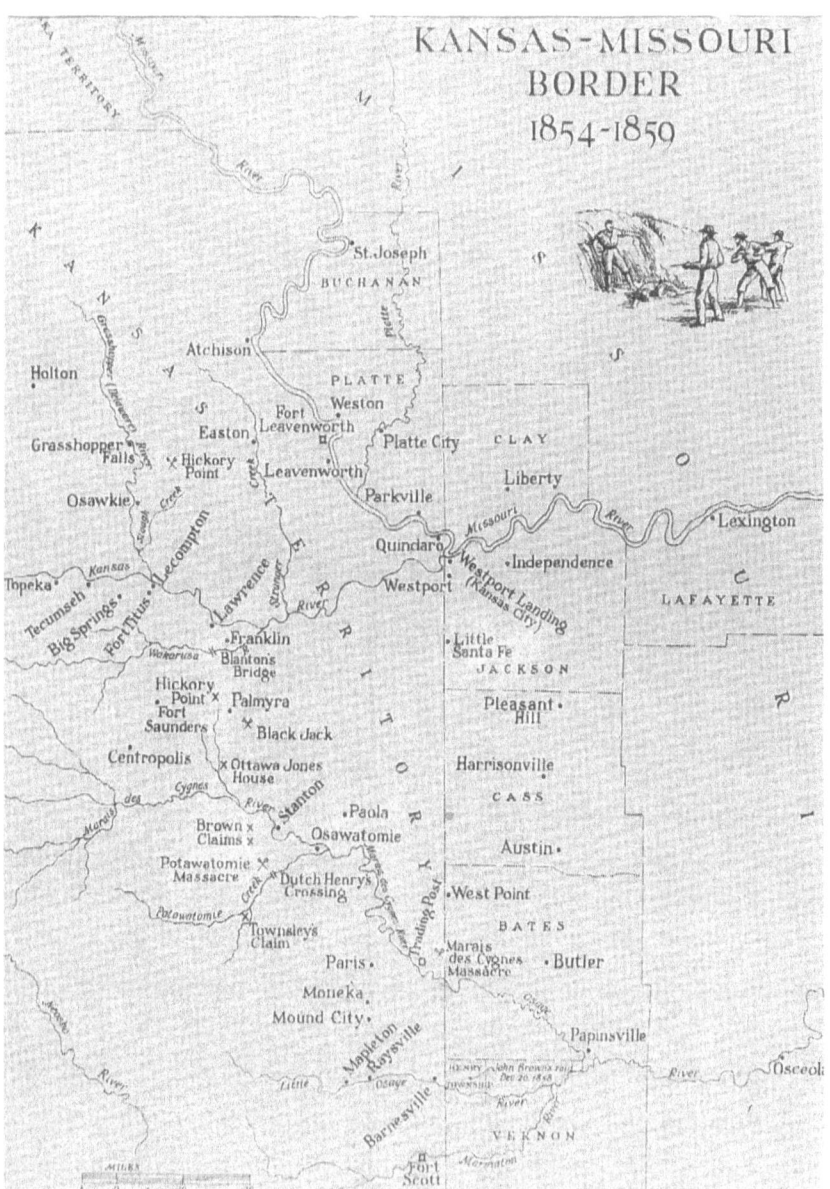

KANSAS-MISSOURI
BORDER
1854-1859

St.Joseph
BUCHANAN
Atchison
Holton
PLATTE
Weston
Fort
Easton Leavenworth
Grasshopper
Falls
Hickory
Point
Leavenworth
Osawkie
Parkville
Liberty
Quindaro
Lexington
Topeka
Kansas
Independence
Westport
Lawrence
Westport Landing
(Kansas City)
LAFAYETTE
Tecumseh
Big Springs
Fort Titus
Franklin
Little
Santa Fe
JACKSON
Wakarusa
Blantons
Bridge
Hickory
Point
Palmyra
Pleasant
Hill
Fort
Saunders
Black Jack
Centropolis
Ottawa Jones
House
Harrisonville
Cygnes
Stanton
CASS
des
Brown x
Claims x
Paola
Osawatomie
Austin
Potawatomie
Massacre
Dutch Henrys
Crossing
West Point
BATES
Potawatomie
Townsleys
Claim
Marais
des Cygnes
Massacre
Butler
Paris
Moneka
Mound City
Papinsville
Mapleton
Raysville
Osceol:
Little
Osage
HENRY John Browns raid
Dec 20 1858
township
River
VERNON
Barnesville
Fort
Scott
Narmaton
MILES

Map by James C. Malin. From Adams. Atlas of American
History/Dictionary of American History, 1E.
© 1978 Gale, a part of Cengage, Inc.
Reproduced by permission.
www.cengage.com/permissions

"Kansas Territory!" my father cried out. "That's the most dangerous place on earth, Ezra." His eyes were as wild as those of a frightened animal and he was breathing heavily.

"You have been the best of fathers, sir," I began, "but I . . . I am not like my brothers, content to stay here in St. Louis."

My father, usually the model of equanimity, rose from his chair, agitation in his voice. "By God, it's a good place to get yourself killed, Ezra."

Nevertheless, into the newly-opened and violent Kansas Territory, I had resolved to go in the spring of 1856, thinking to begin practice as an attorney, since I had studied the law with my father and had my law diploma; besides, I told myself, I reckoned I knew enough law to deal with land claims and the theft of a cow or two. I had already packed my law books along with some clothing in leather cases, and my father, at last, reconciled to my going, settled a small monthly stipend on me—until, he said, I could become established in my profession.

But several days before my departure up the Missouri River to Kansas City, my plans suddenly changed. Since my mother's death when I was six, my father was accustomed to entertaining friends, clients, and business associates at dinners to which my brothers—before they married—and I were occasionally invited. On this warm and breezy April evening, three guests, my father, and I sat around the table after dinner with cigars and port glasses, discussing the slavery question in the Kansas and Nebraska Territories. All the guests, well attired, had mustaches or beards in the fashion of the day; only my father and I were cleanly shaven. The most outspoken of the guests was Russell Downing, editor of the *St. Louis Globe Democrat*, a respected weekly with a wide circulation across Missouri. A stout, sanguine man, perhaps once ginger-haired but now bald, so passionate about politics was he that his face flushed when he spoke.

"The peace in Kansas is as wobbly as a one-legged duck," he spit out, his forehead shining as he gripped the table as though it were about to rise from the floor. My father smiled and gestured toward the decanter of port and Downing, sighing, poured himself another glass.

"Those damned Yankees are the ones stirring up the trouble," growled Arthur Miller, a slave owner and wealthy grain merchant. "Starting those colonies. Abolitionists bringing in wagonloads of Sharps rifles. No reason Kansas shouldn't allow slavery just like Missouri." He leaned back from the table and drew on his cigar. Sitting across from me, Ted Thornberry nodded agreement. He was an ugly man with a bulbous crimson nose that poked out above his full gray mustache.

"The *federals* are the problem, sir. Territorial government so weak that proslavery mobs can exert control," Downing replied, holding up his glass so the candle-light made the port glow like a ruby eye. "Massive fraud in the elections, free-staters beaten or intimidated and kept from the polls. Border Ruffians brought in from Missouri to vote. Two elections stolen, dammit, and a proslavery legislature that will write the constitution for the new state."

My father turned his head, watching the speakers—inspecting them rather. A smile, easy and enigmatic, graced his face, showing keen interest but neither approval nor disapproval of any sentiment uttered. His right hand moved to his cigar, but he did not pick it up. Miller and Thornberry looked at him inquiringly, waiting for him to betray his own view, but Downing, one of my father's closest friends, knew no such revelation would be forthcoming. My father revered the law and served it with devotion but because he dealt with clients of all social classes, religions, and political persuasions, his personal views on many matters were left intentionally opaque. "How does this Kansas business end then?" he asked, turning his head slowly so he took in all of us. Like a Socratic philosopher, he preferred questions.

"Well, I thought *you* might tell us," Thornberry said, "but here's my view. Abolitionists thought slavery would eventually wither up and die but it didn't. So, we have two systems in a state of equilibrium within the Union. Now I say Kansas has to be admitted as a slave state to balance Nebraska—to continue the balance." He held out his hands as though they held apothecaries' weights.

"Nonsense!" said Downing. "If Kansas should vote to enter the Union as a free state or if Fremont or the Republicans win the presidential election, there will be trouble. Some Southern states will secede and there well may be a war."

"Surely enough Missourians with Southern sympathies will settle Kansas to . . .." Thornberry began, but Miller interrupted him.

"But how do we know that?" He reached across the table as if to take Downing's arm. "What does your man in Kansas say, Russell? What will Kansans do?"

"Well, he's usually around Leavenworth, the Salt Creek Valley—where the sentiments are decidedly proslavery," Downing said, lowering his voice to a whisper. "But what's happening in Fort Scott or Lecompton or in Lawrence, where the free-soil settlements are located? Last winter several free-staters were murdered and fortifications were built to protect Lawrence when Border Ruffians threatened. There's already a war brewing in Kansas!"

"Where's the U.S. army?" my father asked. "There *are* dragoons at Fort Leavenworth, aren't there?" He looked at Downing, who lifted his hands in frustration. Everyone fell silent. My father and Thornberry drew on their cigars while Downing looked closely at me.

"Are you certain you want to go to Kansas, practice law there, Ezra?" he asked.

"I'm neutral on the politics, Mr. Downing," I replied. "Perhaps I could bring some order and justice into Kansas through the law." My interlocutor smiled as I said this, perhaps thinking me naïve.

"Perhaps you can," Downing said, looking at my father, who showed his usual half-smile. "Consider this: you could be a correspondent for the *Globe Democrat* while you're getting your law office established—in Lawrence, let's say. For as long as you want to do it. You could send your accounts to my man in Leavenworth and he could telegraph them to me. Or deliver them to the telegraph office in Kansas City—only forty miles away. Yes," he said smiling at me, "we could cover the whole territory. And if you don't find news gathering compatible with your legal work, you can quit in a wink."

The offer was so attractive that I didn't ask about the salary but agreed on the spot to represent the *Globe Democrat*. "Maybe he can write a will or two while he's watching men shoot at each other," my father said sardonically. "Could be lots of legal business there."

After the guests departed, my father spoke again about the dangers of going to Kansas, but I was adamant—and for a reason I had not revealed to my father. My schooling in the East completed, it was intended I join my father's law firm in St. Louis, where my two brothers were already employed, but my education had ignited in me a sense of adventure, and the more I tried to stifle my thoughts the more they smoldered. Washington's headquarters in Cambridge, Faneuil Hall, the Old North Bridge at Concord, Bunker and Breed's Hill, Boston cemeteries where lay the patriots who defied the British and gave their lives for independence: these scenes from my peregrinations down Boston's streets and in the Massachusetts countryside burned in my mind's eye. By comparison, St. Louis seemed dreary and dull. When I was in school, I had read all the latest authors: Hawthorne, Thoreau, Melville, especially Melville, whom I thought as great as Shakespeare, especially his new *Moby Dick*. And so, I returned to St. Louis with a noble passion—to write a novel with the grandeur of *Moby Dick*. But where in a Missouri legal office or the commercial life on the Mississippi River would I find the heroic characters and grand themes I sought. The Western frontier was the answer; there, new Washingtons and Jeffersons, Patrick Henrys and Nathan Hales might be striding across the prairies. So, I would go to Kansas!

In the spring of 1856, it would be no exaggeration to say, the eyes of the nation were fixed on the Kansas Territory. Only two years before, the Kansas-Nebraska Bill had opened the Territory, negating the Missouri Compromise, the set of laws adopted to maintain a balance between slave and non-slave states; henceforth states entering the Union would decide for themselves whether they would allow or forbid slavery—popular sovereignty it was called. Nebraska, adjoining Iowa, it was assumed, would choose to become a free-soil state and Kansas, sharing a boundary with Missouri, would select slavery. If the stakes were high for proponents of slavery and the Southern cause, they were equally high for pioneer farmers moving into Kansas from Iowa, Illinois, and Indiana, who had no wish to protect the rights of slave owners, the stakes higher still for abolitionists in New England, who had seen the institution of slavery strengthen after the invention of the cotton gin and the passage of the Fugitive Slave Law. Now an opportunity to stop its spread presented itself to these Yankee abolitionists, who founded the New England Emigrant Aid Society and established a colony in Lawrence, Kansas Territory, in August 1854. There they met—and evicted by force—proslavery Missouri squatters from land purchased by the Society. And for two years violence steadily escalated.

When I began my journey up the Missouri River, I was exuberant at the prospect of beginning a new profession and new life, but truthfully the trip from St. Louis had made me question my plan to journey to Kansas: sandbars and snags threatened to tear the bottom from our stern-wheeler on a river swollen by spring rain until it seemed nothing but flowing and swirling mud. Had old Charon the Ferryman of Hades been poling his bark against the current, our progress would have been more expeditious, but the tedious journey upriver had afforded me the pleasure of intercourse with my fellow passengers, who sat on deck in the warm May sun, many men having doffed coats and collars and rolled up their shirtsleeves. I spoke with missionaries to the Kansa and Osage Indians, two brothers bound for the California goldfields, a family from Indiana, a sharp-eyed old lady with a parasol, drummers with cases and narrow-brimmed derbies, and people in homespun and straw hats. One man in particular—physically unprepossessing on initial inspection—

proved an amiable companion. With close-set eyes and a pale and lumpy face looking as though it had been carelessly carved from a block of cheese, he stood before me and exclaimed in a voice both rich and melodious: "The name is Thomas Pidgeon and I represent Colt's Fire-Arms Manufacturing Company, maker of the Colt Walker revolver . . . which you must know about." Confessing I did not, I felt the ignorant greenhorn. "You are most fortunate that we have met, sir, for I know more about firearms than anyone in the state of Missouri."

Laughing, I shook the hand he offered me and, after removing his broad-brimmed hat and wiping his face with a handkerchief, down he sat. "I'm Ezra Middleton . . . a correspondent for the *Globe Democrat* of St. Louis, bound for Kansas Territory," I replied.

He emitted a chuckle of delight. "I can't live without my *Globe Democrat*. I must be reading your words each week!" Feeling a profound sense of chagrin, I quickly admitted that I had not yet written a single word that appeared in print. He laughed at my confession and hit me on the shoulder. "Well, *I* may not know everything about firearms either, but allow me to tell you what *you* need to know about Colt revolvers," he said smiling. He began with the 1847 Colt Walker— "finest pistol you ever laid eyes on"—and offered a lesson in revolvers, instruction that Downing insisted I get before entering Kansas. "I'm on my way to Jefferson City now to sell our Dragoon Revolver, Third Model, to gunsmiths there. Lighter with a shorter barrel, less chance of rupture—the model I recommend for your use. Everyone carries a pistol in the Territory."

Later in the day, we went below, where he opened his locked chest to show me several Colt Dragoons, one of which he offered to sell me at wholesale price. "Save you enough to stay a whole week at the Free State Hotel in Lawrence," he exclaimed, chuckling as a deal was struck. I wondered if it be folly to place confidence in someone I scarcely knew, but something in his voice convinced me to trust him. And for the rest of our journey I questioned him about the conflict in Kansas, and, although he seemed only a year or two older than I, recorded his words in my notebook as though he were the wisest sage in Christendom.

When he left the boat in Jefferson City, we spoke of meeting someday in Kansas City, and so parting company he gave me his visiting card with the name of the hotel he frequented.

At last the river packet reached Kansas City, a raw town on the bluff where the Kaw or Kansas River empties into the Missouri, which then bends eastward across the state toward St. Louis and the Mississippi. Kansas City, oddly, is not in Kansas at all but in Missouri, about a mile from the State Line. When I pointed out this curious fact to the old Negro who unloaded my cases at the primitive quay, he shrugged and mumbled "Used to be called Westport Landing," as though his answer clarified everything.

There in Kansas City, I arranged conveyance in a two-wheeled trap south to the town of Westport, from which run the two great highways westward across the empty prairies, the California Road and the Santa Fe Road, which together cross into Kansas before separating about twenty miles from the trailhead of Westport.

Nothing could have been more unlike St. Louis than Westport unless I had gone up the Congo River to colonize the dark heart of Africa. This busy town of shops and buildings was a collection of outfitters, blacksmiths, warehouses for agents in fur and leather, merchants with their crudely painted signs, and grog-shops. Two inns, painted white, stood out among the other buildings. But I was unprepared for the animals—hundreds of mules and oxen to pull the wagons, corral after corral of horses, and pigs and dogs running loose—and covered wagons of all sizes, from huge freight wagons and prairie schooners to small ones carrying the household belongings of a single family, to stage coaches, buckboards, and carriages, as if the whole town had been put on wheels, spinning through the mud and animal droppings, the shouting, the shrieks and bellows of animals, and the malodorous and choking vapors that settled like a ghostly miasma. After a ride down rutted roads, my trap reached the Harris House Hotel, a solid brick structure where a bare-footed Negro boy helped carry my cases. The street was crowded by a variety of humanity—trappers and hunters in fur hats, Negroes and Indians, white men in buckskins, some in flat, broad-brimmed hats and one man in frock coat and dented opera hat, a few women in well-appointed habiliments and others in work dresses and bonnets with a child or two in tow, all moving together as though carried by a turgid current like the one I had so recently left. It seemed as though the continent had been tilted so the population of the eastern states, with all their animals and vehicles, were sliding and tumbling into this Missouri town to be funneled down the two busy highways into Kansas and the vast desert beyond.

Because we needed to cover the forty miles to Lawrence by sundown, I arose before dawn to meet my driver. Sharing a bed with four other men who belched, farted, snored, or noisily used the chamber pot had not been conducive to sleep. Leaving my room on that May morning, I was bone-tired, but my mood changed to one of excitement as we bounced in the dark through Westport's milling animals—oxen, mules, and horses as they snorted and whinnied on being yoked or harnessed. My conveyance was a modest two-mule freight wagon, delivering lumber and goods to Lawrence.

As we rode up the moon-washed road following riders and wagons west across the state line into Kansas, I observed that on the Missouri side the land was neat and fenced and cultivated, the result of thirty years of settlement, fields plowed and planted, fruit trees—apple, I believed—already in blossom, substantial brick or frame houses of prosperous farmers, while on the other side the land was carpeted by tall grass with clumps of trees and an occasional log house. Behind us, the sun climbed through rosy clouds. Birds filled the scented air: larks and red-winged blackbirds chirped and sang to welcome us. We saw an Indian or two watching from the woods as the procession of wagons dropped to the southwest, where they would separate, the California or Oregon Road swinging west to Lawrence and Topeka, the Santa Fe Road continuing to the southwest. The prairie view was breath-taking, like a sea-green ocean rolling toward the shore. However majestic, this country was still primitive and wild. I had seen crude camps outside Westport. Would Lawrence be even worse—shacks, muddy streets with none of the comforts of St. Louis? And could I pursue an untried profession without clean shirts, regular baths, and barbering, I asked myself with a chuckle.

The driver grunted replies to my questions for I had taken out my notebook and pencil to record my first impressions of the Kansas Territory. It disappointed me to learn that he was not a "Yankee abolitionist" but a free-stater from Illinois who settled in Lawrence two years before and conveyed lumber, mail, and occasionally passengers from Kansas City. That I represented the *Globe Democrat* and not a local paper seemed to loosen his tongue and he recounted events in eastern Kansas.

He was Henry Sonnet, who lived in Lawrence, now under threat by Border Ruffians, and thus eager to ascertain the safety of his wife and property. Occasionally he paused, leaned to the side, and spat tobacco juice into the road, then wiped his mouth on his sleeve. Sonnet, I learned as we moved steadily into Kansas, was more than a wagon driver. Realizing that a fast-growing town constantly needed building materials, he had purchased several wagons and hired drivers to carry freight and passengers to Lawrence. Once a week he himself drove the route to Kansas City to arrange for shipments and sign contracts. He had, he confided with a wink and nod, gotten "pretty fair" at bargaining. "You see, I use mules to pull my wagons. Don't wear out like horses. Mules are the thing," he said with a laugh. Sonnet's mule-drawn wagon moved steadily westward, stopping twice for us to relieve ourselves, once to eat cold cornbread.

Surreys, buggies, and carriages—I had ridden in them all on the brick streets and cobblestones in St. Louis and the Boston of my school days and enjoyed the pitch and roll, the sway of the ride. But nothing was like riding in a freight wagon on a dirt road with its ruts and bumps and unseen holes. When I left the hotel, one of the other guests, a greenhorn like me, carrying a carpet bag and wearing a derby, had said," Rode in a freight wagon other day. Like to shook my eyeteeth out." Sonnet, however, seemed oblivious to my distress and kept to his steady pace.

In the late afternoon, two riders galloped toward us. "That's Mick Kelley," Sonnet said, pulling on the reins and rising from his seat to wave down his friends, who slowed their horses to a stop. "What's up?"

"Burned the Free State Hotel!" one rider shouted. "Still burning. Weren't nobody killed. Women weren't bothered." They kicked their horses and rode furiously toward Kansas City.

"Damn! Like I feared," Sonnet muttered, trying to stir his mules into a faster pace. Then speaking nervously, he described events during the winter: volunteers arriving from all quarters, earthworks thrown up on Massachusetts, the main thoroughfare of the town, delivery of a howitzer, and military drills by the able-bodied men, commanded by Dr. Charles Robinson, agent of the Emigrant Aid Society and James Lane, a veteran of the Mexican War. "Governor Shannon finally arranged a truce between the two militias. But it's been worse this spring."

"How so?" I queried. He kept his eyes on the road and his mules.

"Sheriff Jones been trying to arrest some free-staters so I 'spect that's how the Border Ruffians got into town."

"But your wife is safe," I said, looking west to see how much of the day was left. Sonnet nodded. I must have been daft getting into the middle of this deadly dogfight, I thought.

Before we reached Lawrence at sunset, I recognized the acrid smell of burning wood heavy in the air. When we came off the California Road down the main street, I noticed the circular earthworks and in the center of town the still-burning embers of the Free State Hotel, headquarters of the abolitionist movement in Kansas. We reckoned the Border Ruffians had left less than two hours before. Men were pouring water on the ruins of the hotel; others were cleaning debris from the street. Many buildings, looted but not burned, had suffered some damage. As we drove past, Sonnet yelled to men working on a burned log house. "Leona's all right," one old man in a slouch hat shouted, "so's your house and barn."

"We're one street over," Sonnet said, now looking relieved. "That's where we abide. I store the merchandise there." We made our way to Sonnet's barn and stables, where his wife, a sinewy woman of fifty or so, ran out to meet us. The taciturn old free-stater jumped down and whirled his wife off the ground like a girl, kissed her, and then went to unhitch his exhausted mules.

Later, after a meal of rabbit stew, greens, cornbread, and coffee, I told Leona Sonnet I had never been served a better meal in the finest restaurant in St. Louis. Sonnet, who had been sparing of speech on our day-long journey, now became loquacious, calling me "Young Ezra." Even the invasion of the town seemed not to have affected his high spirits. I wondered if they might have lost a child, perhaps a boy who would now have been of my years. When Leona asked if I cared to stay the night, I said that with the Free State Hotel gone I had no place to sleep, then inquired if I might become a regular boarder; she responded affirmatively to my request.

The following day I surveyed the damage on Massachusetts Street, talking to everyone I met and recording my observations in my notebook. In November and December of the preceding year, the Border Ruffians had killed several men. My notes read: *Dec 55 Dow killed (Hickory Point) / Barber killed / free soil militia formed / Rev. Pardee Butler tar and feathers, Atchison / also Phillips / April 20 Sheriff Jones comes with file of dragoons / Jones shot in back, assailant unknown / free state leaders flee early May / 2 free staters murdered by rifle fire Blantons bridge May 19 and 20 / May 21 several hundred Ruffians on Mt Oread. Jones, recovered, leads them in sack of town / Kansas Free Press destroyed and type thrown in the river.* Herald of Freedom *office also looted / drunken Ruffians loot shops / Free State Hotel bombarded by cannon, then kegs of dynamite before interior set ablaze / no one killed except Ruff killed by fallen masonry / hotel owned by Shalor Eldridge total loss / some Ruff wore cords and tassels from curtains of hotel.* Had Robinson, Lane, and the other leaders not fled Lawrence, it seemed certain to everyone I talked to that they would have been lynched or shot.

Although I came to Kansas a dispassionate observer of the political conflict, I was now realizing how difficult remaining uncommitted would be.

By early afternoon I had gathered enough information to write about the sack of Lawrence—my first report for the *Globe*

Democrat—and I proudly signed it *Ezra P. Middleton.* Of course, my name would not appear in the paper. A fair copy was made which I handed to Sonnet's driver, who would carry it to Kansas City to be telegraphed to St. Louis.

The next morning Henry went with me to purchase the horse I would need to pursue stories away from Lawrence. I intended to ride to Lecompton where the territorial legislature, chosen in the fraudulent election, was writing a proslavery constitution and then to Topeka where a free-state assembly was to meet. Although a number of persons had been intimidated or shot at on the roads, as a Missourian I thought I would be safe. Besides I knew the code words to show Southern sympathy: "sound on the goose" or "all right on the hemp."

About noon, with the fury of a tornado, came grim news from Washington, telegraphed to Leavenworth and carried to Lawrence by rider; the previous day, as the bushwhacker mob savaged Lawrence, Senator Charles Sumner—who several days earlier had delivered a scathing speech, "Crime Against Kansas," assailing Southerners—was brutally beaten with a heavy cane on the Senate floor by a South Carolina congressman. Throughout Lawrence news of the attack was met with outrage, women weeping in frustration and men cursing and vowing vengeance. Moreover, Charles Robinson, who in January of 1856, was chosen "governor" of the extralegal free-soil government and leader of the Emigrant Aid Society, after leaving town to raise funds in the East, had been captured in Missouri and was to be taken to Lecompton to stand trial. The Southern case seemed to be prevailing and with Robinson gone the free-soil movement seemed about to collapse.

One by one Henry's friends gathered beneath a newly-leafed young maple near the barn where two logs provided seating in front of Leona's kitchen garden: corn almost two feet high, melon vines, beans, and onions all in neat well-tended rows. Two had jugs of whiskey and Henry took out a plug of tobacco, which one by one they attacked with their bowie knives. One small man, missing some teeth, dribbled tobacco juice down his gray beard and many of them spat when they spoke of the bushwhackers. "Goddamn pukes," one thin, hatchet-faced fellow growled. As they talked, I began to realize that their interest was not so much the ill-treatment of Negro slaves but the fear that slavery's establishment in Kansas would deprive them of their political rights; these unkempt, hard-handed men in their pants of homespun linsey were not abolitionists but shrewd farmers who saw the institution of slavery threatening the value of their labor and their emoluments. Consequently, I wondered whether circumstances would inevitably draw them into an alliance with abolitionists like James Lane and the more militant of his party.

"We obeyed the territorial government, even if it were bogus," exclaimed the broad-shouldered blacksmith from whom I had bought my horse. "Now things have gone to smash!"

"Our hour of trial is come," snarled a black-bearded farmer I knew only as 'John.' "That posse burned our town were Missourians. President Pierce favors the South, so does Governor Shannon and Sheriff Jones. The turds want to exterminate us like vermin!" The knot of settlers yelled and hooted. A few brandished long-bladed knives. They roared in frustration like a pack of baying dogs, and a phrase from Shakespeare came to my mind: *let slip the dogs of war.* Antony says it.

Turning, I walked back through the barn, intending to stop at the privy, when I noticed a wooden crate, perhaps a box that had been in the wagon which had brought me to Lawrence. I pried loose a board and, to my surprise, saw half-hidden under surveying instruments a dozen or so rifles. So, Henry has been carrying more than lumber, a dangerous sideline with a bushwhacker militia patrolling the Wakarusa Valley. As I turned, I found him standing calmly before me, a smile on his face.

"Part of my business, Ezra," Henry said.

"Are these the Sharps rifles I've been hearing so much about?" His smile broadened. "Why did that posse want to confiscate them, Henry?"

"You see, they're breech loading—not muzzle loading—fast firing, and long range. Better than anything the bushwhackers got. Supplied by the Aid Companies." He looked at me intently. "Kept the Ruffians from over-running Lawrence—except for two days ago."

"Well, I intend to write about them. Heard they're known as
'Beecher's Bibles'—after Reverend Henry Ward Beecher. Also
heard he passed the collection plate to purchase Sharps rifles
for recruits and sent them west in boxes marked 'Bibles.' The rifles, I mean, not the recruits," I explained laughing and Sonnet
smiled. It confused me that he would trust me with his secret.

"I 'spect some newspaper fellow made that up." Henry's high-
pitched laugh filled the barn. "Let me tell you how it is, Ezra,
and you can write it up. These rifles are to protect our town, but
we won't use them against the dragoons from Leavenworth or
the U.S. Marshals or even Sheriff Jones' posse. And we got to
keep *our* hotheads from doing anything to make things worse—
like Jim Lane or old Osawatomie Brown. We're still under
threat, but we don't want to *start* a war here in Kansas."

CHAPTER TWO

To learn about human nature, my father often said, turn to the pages of Mr. William Shakespeare. His drama is the mirror of nature. The history plays and Roman tragedies were my father's particular favorites, and he loved the plays with trial scenes—*The Merchant of Venice,* the last act of *Measure for Measure* with its themes of justice and mercy, and the trial of Hermione in *The Winter's Tale.* The contrasts between characters fascinated him as well: Hamlet and Laertes, Brutus and Antony, Prince Hal and Hotspur. Of course, quotations from the Bard were a staple of my father's courtroom oratory, delivered with an actor's rhetorical flourishes. Would that our discussions could provide insights into the minds and motives of the grim players on the Kansas stage.

Needing to learn more about the leaders of the free-state party, I recalled that Henry Sonnet had spoken of the fiery abolitionist called Captain John Brown, who had appeared in Lawrence in December 1855, when four or five hundred Border Ruffians threatened the town. Arriving from Osawatomie, thirty-five miles to the south with a troop of about twenty, including his four sons, all supplied with navy revolvers and heavy broadswords, Brown's free-state militia—the Liberty Guards—bolstered up the defenses and a truce was arranged by Governor Shannon, much to the old man's disgust, according to Henry. Now, after a bitterly cold winter, hostilities had heated up with the warmer weather as Brown continued to call for extreme action against the bushwhackers and the Federal troops who seemed to protect them.

Determined to visit Brown's Station near Osawatomie, I conferred with Henry, who suggested I await word that most of the Missouri bushwhackers had left the area south of Lawrence along the Wakarusa. The morning before my intended departure to see John Brown, I took a basket of clothes to be washed and visited the barbershop for a bath and shave, realizing I should have reversed these activities since Mrs. Pierce, the laundress, had a buxom blonde daughter of about my age called Ginny. But in the evening came shocking news from south of the Wakarusa: near Dutch Henry's Crossing on Pottawatomie Creek, two nights earlier, a series of brutal and gruesome killings of five proslavery settlers had occurred, apparently reprisals for the sack of Lawrence and the beating of Senator Sumner in Washington. The perpetrators were John Brown, four of his sons, and two others, who had with broadswords hacked to death their victims.

Rumor has swift feet and a thousand voices as Shakespeare shows in his *Henry IV* plays and by noon everyone in town had heard the report. The murders horrified most, some thought the act of vengeance justified, if excessively bloody, and others feared this and other acts of the past week would breed a sanguinary progeny. "Blood will have blood," I heard more than one person say. I wondered if the use of the cutlasses was suggested by the vicious murder of free-stater Reese Brown by a band of drunken Kickapoo Rangers, who hacked their victim to death with hatchets, an event of the January past still remembered with anger in Lawrence. I quickly wrote a report based on what I thought was the most reliable version of the attack and asked Henry if one of his riders could carry it to the telegraph office in Kansas City.

In the next few days accounts reached us of frightened proslavery settlers fleeing the Wakarusa Valley and free-staters forced to leave the proslavery stronghold of Leavenworth. Bands of fighters from both sides were now hunting one another in the woods, and local newspapers fueled the fear and hysteria. Of course, the two Lawrence papers had been silenced but proslavery papers like the *Squatter Sovereign* and the *Kickapoo Kansas Pioneer* were filled with exaggerated accounts of the incidents and inflammatory rhetoric. Despite the danger, I was determined to talk to Osawatomie Brown.

With my saddlebags filled with johnnycakes and carrying my revolver, I rode south to Palmyra, fifteen miles in distance. At nightfall, having seen no trace of Brown in an afternoon of hunting, I tied up my horse and ate some of my johnnycakes; putting down my blanket, I was more afraid of rattlesnakes curling up beside me in the night than bushwhackers, yet I made no fire. Before falling asleep, I thought of my father and my brothers with their nubile wives in their soft beds in St. Louis.

On the second day of my quest, as I walked my horse through the woods, I followed a road that seemed but a mere memory of an older road, perhaps a trail left by Indians or deer. The air smelled as sweet as newly-churned butter, the sunlight mottled by the intense green of new leaves. Spider webs shimmered before me in the morning sun like strands of silver wire, unbroken by a passerby. The woods had fallen silent: no birds chattered or sang in the branches above my head. Then I heard a noise behind me, a footfall. Turning, I faced a black-bearded man holding a revolver aimed at my chest.

"I'm Middleton of the *St. Louis Globe Democrat*," I said, holding my hands away from the revolver stuck in my waistband. "I'm looking for Captain John Brown."

"Why do you want him?" He took a step or two toward me, frowning. He was about my age, simply dressed, his hair wild and his beard in need of grooming.

"To talk to him for my paper," I answered. "Our readers would like to know his views on Kansas matters."

"Well, he may be able to accommodate you. I'm Salmon Brown." A smile crossed his face. "He likes you news scribes, but I need to keep your firearm for a while. Many people wish him harm, you know."

"What do you know about the Pottawatomie attack?" I asked, choosing my words carefully.

"I got nothing to say." After a moment's silence, he added sourly: "You have to ask my father."

Handing over my revolver, I followed Salmon Brown through the woods along an indistinct path that led to a clearing. Here several sentinels with rifles casually stood guard. Then I saw an old man who could have been only the choleric abolitionist, Brown. He was older than I expected with a grim and weathered face, dark hair streaked with gray, and several weeks' growth of beard. His face showed no emotion but his eyes, lustrous as polished metal, suggested a keen intelligence and sense of purpose. "Who have we here?" he asked his son, his voice a reedy tenor.

"Writes for the *Globe Democrat,* he says," the younger Brown answered. Old Brown was simply dressed: dark coat and vest, kerchief at his throat. Now I noticed that the old man's toes protruded from his boots and I clenched my teeth so as not to laugh.

"May I ask some questions, sir?" My voice sounded forced but did not crack. He nodded, gestured toward a log, and sat down on one end. "What can you tell our readers about the attack on Pottawatomie?" I took out the notebook and a pencil from my pocket.

"There is a terrible evil in this land," he said, leaning forward. "A monstrous evil which is slavery. An evil which must be extirpated—destroyed root and branch." He spoke precisely with little emotion and his eyes seemed both cold and fiery at the same time. I remembered Henry Sonnet saying that Brown had the eyes of a rattlesnake about to strike. I thought his eyes more like those of a raptor—a hawk or an eagle. Perhaps I could see nobility in his countenance too.

"It's being called a massacre," I said, trying to keep my voice calm. "Unarmed, innocent people—men and boys."

"Not innocent," he said, his voice low, pointing at me with a gnarled finger. "No, not innocent! They were tainted by the institution of slavery. Hands stained also with the blood of free state martyrs." His voice began to rise. "But the slave masters will be stricken with pestilence like Pharaoh's Egyptians, who held in bondage the children of Israel. Jehovah has not forgotten the people held in slavery—the Negro, I mean. His right hand is Majestic in strength."

He was on his feet now, pacing in front of me, his eyes, wilder now, never leaving my face. Muscles in his face twitched as though fierce passions burned within. Listening to him, I thought of Shakespeare but realized that it was Melville who had created a character so obsessed: Ahab. I half-remembered a line from the novel that the Whale was evil personified. Perhaps how Brown saw slavery: the sum of all evil. It was disturbing to see his passions flare from calm to explosive anger in seconds, like kerosene thrown on a fire.

"People say you killed five men and boys at Pottawatomie. Is that right, Captain?"

"The *prophets* say the Almighty has many arrows for his enemies. God has called me to purge the land of this evil, which can only be done by the shedding of blood—the shedding of blood! I have heard the voice of the Lord." He paused. "I am an old man and the time allotted to me may be short, so I must ever be doing His work while I have breath." He turned around and walked toward a fire where members of his company were roasting a pig. "Pardon my manners," he said as calmly and politely as a host greeting a dinner guest. "You must be hungry. One of my sons will cut you some meat of the pig. I must attend to my men." His weathered face broke into a smile and he nodded and walked away.

Realizing I would get no more from Brown, I joined six or eight men around the fire and accepted a piece of pork, which I devoured quickly since for two days I had eaten nothing but johnnycakes. I sat on the ground with Salmon and another brother whom I believed was Owen. "This is a military company, isn't it?" I observed.

Salmon laughed. "Except we pray together twice a day and can't cuss in camp. He's a Calvinist." Then he said fiercely: "We intend to wipe out the Missouri bushwhackers. Carry the fight to them. Not wait around to be attacked and burned out."

"But the dragoons from Ft. Leavenworth want to stop the fighting—on both sides. Will *you* tell me about the purpose of the Pottawatomie attack?"

It was Owen who answered. "Don't matter," he said. "Now the name John Brown makes the Missourians shit in their pants." All of them laughed.

"Things have changed," Salmon said, suddenly becoming solemn. "Pottawatomie . . . we're all troubled by it. That's my brother Frederick over there," he said pointing to the husky auburn-haired man pacing back and forth near the horses, talking to himself and gesturing. "He can't forget the blood." So, this was the brother whom Henry Sonnet had said was not quite right in the head. And now he had new demons to fight.

"We've told our father we must never do that again," Owen said. "But we *will* use the scepter of Justice to free the slaves." He looked at me and smiled. "We can offer you coffee, but no sugar. We break up the beans with a rock." He laughed, walked to the fire, and brought back a tin cup of hot coffee. "No more questions," he said politely.

"Just one more, if you don't mind," I said. Owen and Salmon stood before me as I rose to take the proffered cup. "Why are you here now?" They exchanged glances but before either could answer, a sunburnt man in a straw hat, his pantaloons stuffed inside his red-topped boots, walked up and extended his hand to me.

"James Redpath," he announced. "Perhaps I can answer that." I introduced myself and discovered him to be a Scotsman and, like myself, a writer. "I've been with this company for a few days. They've been looking for Henry Pate's territorial militia— Southern bushwhackers, really." It surprised me to see Redpath dressed like everyone in Brown's company, although I don't suppose I expected him to wear a kilt and a sporran.

He looked at the brothers. "Sorry, boys, but Pate captured John and Jason two days ago." John, of course, was John Brown, Junior. "All I know is they were turned over to the U.S. Calvary, who will probably take them to Lecompton. At least they weren't lynched." He shook his head.

About an hour later, shortly after the sun went down, Brown and his company left the camp, Redpath and I following as observers but carrying our revolvers. Through the night, Brown's free-state militia had advanced silently toward the Missourians' camp. When the sun came up, they were in position and around nine o'clock Brown signaled and his men ran down a hill toward Pate's Southerners. I could hear the old man yelling, "Aim low! Don't waste ammunition." Brown's company had been joined by another free-state company commanded by young Samuel Shore, whose twenty-five or thirty men were twice Brown's number. Pate's men, waiting in the tall prairie grass along the old Santa Fe Road, began firing and Shore's men returned fire.

Redpath and I tried to stay behind the tree line so we could see the whole battlefield in relative safety. For almost two hours the firing continued with casualties on both sides. Pate had drawn four supply wagons together to form a breastwork, behind which a ravine sloped down to Black Jack Springs. In horror, I saw one of Pate's men take a ball in the jaw and roll on the ground in agony. I had never witnessed such an act of bloodshed before.

Seeing some of Pate's men who had sought cover in the ravine trying to sneak away, Brown ordered two of his men to shoot only at the enemy's horses and mules. Now the screams of terrified and dying animals caused sudden panic among the bushwhackers and more of them attempted to slip away. With Brown's company still outnumbered two or three to one and the issue uncertain, Brown's demented son, Frederick, galloped out onto the open prairie in view of both sides, waving his sword and shouting "Father, we have them surrounded!" The ruse worked. As Brown advanced with drawn revolver down the ravine, the Missourians, hands in the air, under a white flag, came out from the scrub oak to surrender, twenty-six of them, several badly wounded. Redpath and I raced to the bottom of the ravine. Brown's small company—Captain Shore's men had fled during the battle—disarmed the prisoners and offered them water. Brown's plan, I believe, was to exchange Pate's men for the free-state men imprisoned in Lecompton, including Brown's two sons, but, of course, Brown had no authority to arrange such an agreement—he was wanted for the Pottawatomie incident and was thought to have a price on his head—so I assumed that the U.S. Army would just take the prisoners from Brown and later set them free.

After bidding Redpath farewell, instead of returning to Lawrence, I mounted my horse and set off for the telegraph office in Kansas City down the Santa Fe Road. This was the day so many had dreaded, the first battle between free-state and proslavery forces in the Kansas Territory. It was a day I would remember, June 2, 1856. In my account, I would call it the Battle of Black Jack after the nearby hamlet.

CHAPTER THREE

The morning after telegraphing Downing my account of the battle near Black Jack Springs, I took a buggy back to Westport to get my horse from the stableman who cares for Sonnet's mules and set out up the California Road for Lawrence, the route I had taken on the day the town was sacked two weeks before. In my youthful *naivete`*, I thought myself a changed man. Had I not seen men killed in battle and heard of neighbors hacked to death for their political opinions? Downing had predicted that the peace, such as it was, would break down—and now it had. Newspapers across the country were calling the last two months of 1855 "The Wakarusa War," a misleading hyperbole since the Missouri Border Ruffians, who frequently threatened Lawrence and killed the occasional free-state settler, had not laid waste the town or murdered its inhabitants.

As I rode into Lawrence at the end of the day, the damage to the town was no longer evident— broken windows and doors had been replaced, the ruins of the Free State Hotel the sole reminder of the wrath of the Missourians. Since I was now well known, many citizens waved and shouted greetings, asking me about the military action near Palmyra the previous day. I was about to unsaddle my horses when Leona Sonnet came running around the barn and hugged me tightly, then stood on tip-toe to kiss my face, saying, "We were worried, Ezra," until overcome with joy she could say no more. I am not ashamed to say that tears came to my eyes.

As I was eating a piece of cold cornbread and jam, Sonnet burst into the kitchen. "Heard you was back," he said, grabbing my hand. "Did you find Old Osawatomie?"

"Found him and watched him beat Pate's Border Ruffians in a battle, a real battle," I said with enthusiasm. "And I wrote it up for my paper. Just got back from the telegraph in Kansas City."

"Dammit," Henry said. "That's worth more than a monkey show. Sure is." Leona gave him a cup of coffee and he tapped his cup against mine as if he were making a toast. "Glad to see you whole," he said growing solemn. "That reminds me . . ." He left the kitchen, returning immediately with the saddlebags in which he carried the mail from Kansas City. "Some for you, Ezra," he said laughing. "In fact, most of it's for you." There were several issues of the *Globe Democrat,* one of the *Missouri Democrat* (a proslavery St. Louis paper which Downing had sent me), a letter from Downing and one from my father. One of the issues of the *Globe Democrat* had my account of the sack of Lawrence. This I handed to Leona while I sat down to read my two letters.

I was pleased my father did not chide me for neglecting to set up a legal office; in fact, it was a slight shock to be reminded that lawyering was part of my original plan. He conveyed greetings from my brothers and warned me to sail clean of the "madman" John Brown, referring me to the *Missouri Democrat*'s exaggerated description of Brown as a "devil incarnate." Downing's letter, I was amused to note, instructed me to set a watch on Brown. Had I the hundred eyes of Argus, I would be hard pressed to find Brown's militia again in the scrub oak of eastern Kansas, but I was certain our paths would continue to cross. In the meantime, I planned to ride to Lecompton, the capital of the proslavery territorial government, only six or seven miles to the west.

Lecompton was smaller than Lawrence, composed of rough-board houses, land-offices, and many whiskey-saloons, at one of which some loafers were congregating. Unlike Lawrence, which was backed by the steep treeless escarpment called Mount Oread or, in jest, the Devil's Backbone or Hogback Ridge, Lecompton was on a bluff and without character. I asked one of the idle locals about the location of the territorial prison, which I assumed would be an imposing building. He gave a snort and spat tobacco juice at the feet of my horse: "Where we put 'em that wants to abolitionize Kansas," he said with a cackle, pointing to a barn with a few barred windows. As I rode up to the building, I was shocked to note that the inmates were lightly guarded, not locked into cells or rooms. Sara Robinson, I had read in the *Globe Democrat*, had called her husband's prison the "Bastille on the Kansas prairies," which was scarcely the case. Indeed, most of the prisoners seemed to be allowed to roam without hindrance the area outside the barn and near the privy. Several approached as I dropped from my horse.

"Charles Robinson of the free-state government of Kansas," said a fine-looking man with high forehead and spectacles. "Welcome to the Lecompton Territorial Gaol." He laughed and shook my hand. He had the bearing of a schoolmaster; his eyes suggested wariness.

As I introduced myself, he examined me closely. "Is it not dangerous to call yourself that, sir?" I asked.

"Well, I spoke that partly in jest. I have been indicted for repudiating the Territorial Legislature's authority and now I think I shall be accused of treason—so they can hang me." He took me by the elbow and led me into a shady spot next to the gaol, where we sat in weathered wooden chairs.

"Is promoting a free-state government an act of treason?" I asked.

"Mr. Middleton, the territorial government has held two elections. In both, there was massive fraud: Kansas citizens intimidated or beaten or shot, Missourians allowed to vote"—he stopped, then said with a smile— "many times. So, having been elected in a totally free election, I believe I might even call myself *the* governor." Before I could respond, a man with a bushy black beard approached and Robinson motioned to him. "That is John Brown, Jr.," Robinson said softly. "Had a bad time, poor fellow. First, the killings at Pottawatomie—which he wasn't a part of— and then the brutal treatment after his capture—chained, abused as a prisoner. He mumbles and at times his eyes flash like a mad man's. Best not to ask him about Pottawatomie."

"I know Captain Brown," I said to John Junior, who now stood before us. "A man of principle. I admire his courage." I paused to see how this was received, but his look told me nothing. "I'm a correspondent for the *St. Louis Globe Democrat*."

"Father is zealous in God's righteous labor. Our family joins him . . . soldiers in the holy cause." Brown looked about in confusion and Robinson led him to a chair.

"Do you want for anything here," I asked, "except for your freedom, of course." Dr. Robinson smiled and touched Brown on the knee.

"The territorial militia guards us, and the dragoons who support them are intended to keep the Missourians from us, but who can say how safe we are." Henry Sonnet had called Robinson patient and cautious, qualities which I believe I saw in him. "Eight of the free-state party are here, myself included, whom the Missourians want to kill," Robinson said this matter-of-factly.

"Our friends bring us fruit and cakes, books, and we have church services," Brown said gleefully. "We have music too. Like a Fourth of July picnic." For the moment he seemed to have to forgotten Pottawatomie.

"Just so. But no, our friends from Lawrence and Topeka have not forgotten us," Robinson added. "They write to Congress and the President. My wife is busy with speeches and letters—an indefatigable one, she is."

Since Brown had shown some interest in our conversation, I cautiously asked him, "Why is your father so zealous to end the sufferings of the Negro?"

"Father taught us to fear God and hate slavery. Operated fugitive slave stations in Ohio and Pennsylvania before we came to Kansas. Do you know the Subterranean Pass Way?" Brown asked looking back and forth at us.

"Yes," I said. "The Underground Railroad. Carries fugitive slaves to safety. Was your father a conductor?"

Brown nodded eagerly. "I did it too, even here in Kansas. Not a sin to steal slaves from slaveholders, is it?" As he talked, he seemed more alert and at ease. The wild look had all but disappeared from his eyes. Since I could not ask about Pottawatomie, I asked about his childhood with Old Brown and my interlocutor looked pensive and did not speak for several moments.

"When I was a lad of ten years, I worked in my father's tannery but was sometimes indolent," he finally said, speaking rapidly. "He had an account book to record my faults or debits, to each of which was assigned a certain number of lashes that could be canceled by credits—setting good examples for my

younger brothers, acts of industry. One day my father sat down
with me and went through the ledger deed by deed, asking if the
audit was fair. Tearfully I acknowledged that it was, and he said
it was time for a reckoning. So, I walked to a pile of hides and
bent over. Although he had allowed me to keep on my trousers,
the pain when he hit me with the beech switch was sharp. At
eight the blows stopped, far short of the twenty-five due me.

When I looked back at him, he had removed his coat and
shirt. He handed me the switch and himself bent over the hides.
'Seventeen more lashes are due,' he said, 'and I will take them
for you since I have failed to teach you your duties.' He instructed me to hit him and with each blow commanded: 'Harder!
Harder!' as the switch bit into his bare flesh, beads of blood
trickling down his back." Brown stopped, tears in his eyes as he
finished his story. "My father taught me to walk in the path of
righteousness. I will never abandon the struggle to eradicate
slavery." He gave me a bow and walked back toward the barn.

"You see a devout but troubled man," Robinson said. "For
some, the struggle is wiping out slavery. For others—like myself—the struggle is about freedom. Yes, for Negroes but white
men too. Freedom to shape the institutions that govern us. It is
a great cause, Mr. Middleton, like that which our forefathers
faced in the East in Colonial times. *Our* cause is to build the
New Jerusalem here in the pleasant land of Kansas."

Since the afternoon was wearing on and storm clouds seemed
to be moving in from the west, I bid Dr. Robinson farewell, saying I would carry his salutations to Henry Sonnet, and set off for
Topeka, a free-state bastion almost twenty miles to the west,
where the California Road crossed the Kansas River. As I rode
under the darkening afternoon sky, I reflected on my time with
Dr. Robinson and Brown, Junior. Robinson was a man of intelligence and pragmatism, moreover a man whose passions did not
rule him—a rarity on the Kansas plains, where the basest or
most volatile aspects of character seemed to dominate. Would
Brown recover from the physical suffering and mental strife he
had endured? And what of Robinson's incarceration at Lecompton—was it a "durance vile," as Sara Robinson had called it, and
could the free-state cause survive without the doctor to lead it?

After I had ridden an hour or so, rain fell, and I unrolled my oil-skin, endeavoring to keep as dry as possible. Shortly after dark I saw the lights of Topeka and found the small hotel which Sonnet had recommended, if that word can convey his half-hearted endorsement. Still, I had a dry bed and my horse clean, dry hay.

The next day I waded through Topeka's mud to find the representatives of the extralegal free-state assembly which, leaderless, had begun meeting in March to write a constitution that forbade slavery. I wanted to meet James Henry Lane, who had a house in Lawrence but was frequently engaged in politics elsewhere. Robinson had told me he thought Lane might be in Topeka, but that information turned out to be wrong. Nevertheless, what I gleaned in Topeka made the trip worthwhile and so two days later I retraced my steps across the beautiful open plains to Lawrence.

As I rode east that morning, the sun bright in my face, I was thinking that a person who has not traveled on the prairie cannot imagine its beauty. With few trees—and these usually growing in the ravines which occasionally cut into a landscape covered in knee-high grass—the horizon was empty and wide, stretching for miles.

The prairie is not flat but undulating and sinuous, as though huge serpents from ancient times moved uneasily beneath the surface. I could imagine the horizon curving away like a globe, although I knew from my university studies that could not be the case. Above me in a sky azure and cloudless soared meadowlarks and a hawk, and in the distance, a string of white prairie schooners seemed to float toward me through a sea of grass.

Arriving in Lawrence and leaving my muddy horse under the care of Sonnet's Negro stable boy, Isaac, I entered the kitchen, where Henry and Leona were finishing their supper. "Woo! A mud hen," he said with a cackle.

"Seen mud aplenty," I laughed, brushing at my dirty pants. "Been to Lecompton and Topeka. Dr. Robinson sends his regards." Leona fixed me some supper and Henry poured me a cup of coffee.

"Quiet here, but I heard that Brown's militia is on the move and some Lawrence free-staters shot up Franklin. Colonel Sumner and his cavalry been trying to keep order. Cavalry's as useless as teats on a boar hog."

"Get him the telegram, you old fool," Leona shouted at Henry, who laughed and left the room, returning with an envelope.

"Likes what I wrote about John Brown—Downing, I mean," I said, waving the telegram at them. "He says the whole country wants to know about him. The 'mad abolitionist.' Downing's sending newspapers by mail."

"Eat some supper, Ezra," Leona said. "I can heat some water for a bath." Thanking her, I ate.

"The only hot food I've had in days . . . except for a piece of pork in John Brown's camp." Then I remembered a bit of news I had for Henry. "I heard there's talk of a free-state celebration on the Fourth of July in Topeka."

"Lots of patriotic speeches, I bet. Just what the rabble-rousers like Brown and Lane need to start trouble with the dragoons," Sonnet said, looking worried and glancing at Leona. "Territorial government won't let that happen. Governor Shannon'll send for the U.S. troops."

"There could be fireworks," I said, trying to be humorous. The three of us exchanged glances but neither of them laughed.

CHAPTER FOUR

The next morning, I awoke coughing and feeling poorly. Seeing me stagger into the kitchen, Leona sent me to the parlor and brought me a posset, sweetened with honey and laced with whiskey. "You should stay here today," she said firmly. "A catarrh, I suspect, caught out in the rain. No trips today." She said to her husband: "We might call the doctor—old Mortuary Morris will be in town."

"I ain't getting old Mortuary Morris for Ezra," Sonnet said and laughed. "Wouldn't let him treat my mules, would I?"

"Is he an undertaker too?" I asked between coughs.

"No, does introduce some of his patients *to* the undertaker though," Sonnet exclaimed and laughed again.

That day and the next I spent under the care of Leona Sonnet, and with fried eggs and whiskey possets I quickly improved. It was pleasant to rest and answer her questions as she came in between chores: Did I miss St. Louis? Had I left a sweetheart there? How long might I stay in Lawrence? Had I met any girls here? When she was satisfied with my answers, she talked about her life with Henry and the birth of their only child—a boy—twenty years before and his death from cholera. "The Lord giveth and the Lord taketh away," she said, sadness in her voice, and I wondered if she and Henry often talked about their loss as they struggled with the threats and hardships of the Kansas frontier.

And threats there were, threats aplenty. John Brown's militia was still in the field along with another free-state company led by Sam Walker, and James Lane was rumored to be raising troops in Nebraska. Because of the danger, crops could not be harvested and in the unseasonably wet weather, they rotted in the fields. Meanwhile, as the Fourth of July approached, my task was to collect the information Downing had asked for, using a phrase now appearing in newspapers across the country: "*Bleeding Kansas.*" When I had visited his camp, Brown confided that like the Prophets in the Holy Book he and his sons would make their dwelling with the serpents of the rock and the wild beasts of the wilderness until slavery had been wiped out in Kansas. Now, I discovered, he waited on the banks of the Shunganunga Creek, south of Topeka, ready to attack either bushwhackers or the dragoons—the U.S. cavalry—should the territorial government try to break up the free-state celebration on the Fourth.

Henry and I were up before dawn so we could arrive in Topeka by noon. Leona wished to accompany us, desiring to hear the patriotic speeches and the bands and to see the fireworks, but Henry gently but firmly insisted she stay at home—with good reason, I thought. Assuming that the territorial government would not allow the free-state celebration, I was certain that Federal troops would be called and without Dr. Robinson to control the crowd in Topeka I feared that a deadly clash with the cavalry was possible. But in the end Henry relented and Leona climbed aboard the buggy with a basket of victuals. "Can't say 'no' to the woman, you see," Henry mumbled and laughed.

On reaching Topeka, we saw wagons, buggies, and riders entering an already crowded town, feverish with excitement. The day was hot, and fingers of heat rose from the hard-packed dirt road. Bands played patriotic tunes, several local military companies were in uniform, flags and banners were being waved and women promenaded, dressed in their finery. Inside the legislative chamber, speakers delivered fiery speeches in honor of the country's eightieth anniversary and the free-state cause. At the campground, I learned that Federal troops had reached Topeka the previous day and Colonel Edwin Sumner—a cousin of the Massachusetts senator beaten on the Senate floor, the very officer who had taken custody of Pate's defeated bushwhackers at Black Jack Springs—was waiting to deploy his troops. Sumner's command comprised five companies of cavalry—perhaps a thousand dragoons—and two pieces of artillery, loaded, I was told, with grapeshot. Facing them were two companies of local militia on the broad avenue that stretched to the hall where the illegal

free-state legislature had been meeting. As the mass of specta-
tors slowly backed away, I was left, close enough I could touch
the horses and hear their breathing and whickering. The militia
drummers continued to play as the dragoons, their sabers flash-
ing in the sun, slowly walked their horses until they were an
arm's length from the militiamen. The two sides uneasily faced
each other. Then Colonel Sumner dismounted, his military
brass jingling, and boldly strode into the legislative chamber,
and I followed him to the doorway. Despite the heat, Sumner
looked crisp and resplendent, as calm as though he were choosing a partner at a dance.

"I am called to perform the most painful duty of my entire life,
for I am here to disperse this assembly and to inform you that
you cannot meet. If you do not disperse, I shall use the forces
available to me to carry out my orders," Sumner announced in
an even and forceful voice. To my great surprise, the chamber
was almost empty, the orators and their audience having leaped
from the windows and like rabbits bounded across the lawn.

The better part of valor is discretion, Shakespeare's humorous
warrior Falstaff says to justify his cowardice, a line I was
tempted to share with the Colonel, who spun around, brushed
past me, and, expressionless, returned to his men. A number of
the women, whose colorful parasols shielded them from the sun,
stood before the hall in dismay, searching for husbands hiding
in the bushes. Already like a web, my story of anticipation and
ironies was knitting itself together in my mind. I scratched down
a few details in my notebook before looking for Leona. Already
the crowd was dispersing and the free-state government in Topeka had been put down, perhaps dismembered for good—
without a struggle. Although many people returned dejectedly to
their wagons, others in choler and frustration called out "bun-
kum" and "claptrap" at the dragoons and shook their fists.
Everyone seemed to have forgotten the evening's fireworks display.

Leona and I found Henry waiting by his horses, still in har-
ness in the shade of the livery stable. "Guess we should go
home," he said. "We got a long trip, but at least no one got killed
today."

As we traveled back on the steamy California Road in the afternoon sun, Henry offered us his canteen and said: "Got some news for you, Ezra," and made certain he had my attention. "Saw a friend of Jim Lane's. Says he's assembled an army and should be moving through Nebraska now." He bit into the apple that Leona offered him. "Your editor might want to know about that. Can't be sure, but he could be heading for Lawrence."

"At last I can talk to the famous Lane," I responded.

"Famous? A right scoundrel, I'd say," Henry snorted, urging the horses forward. "Oh, he's a good military man but he's unscrupulous and ambitious."

"No telling what his army will be like. Maybe as rowdy as the Missouri Ruffians," Leona added.

Chewing on his apple, Henry said: "Lane preaches abolitionism, but I heard he tried to buy a female slave after his wife left him." He glanced at his wife. "Him and Robinson are bitter enemies, you see, but Robinson may need him, if he ever gets out of Lecompton."

When we reached Lawrence later in the day, we discovered that a report about the free-state fiasco had preceded us as well as a rumor that Lane's army—for so it was now being called— had been joined by John Brown and the fiery Sam Walker. When I composed my account for Downing, I speculated that the most radical elements in Kansas now seemed to govern the free-state movement.

In the next few days, members of Lane's militia drifted into town, heavily armed. When I met Lane, an affable sandy-haired man with eyes so dark they seemed black, I sensed a mercurial nature with much restless energy and resolve. Since he knew I wrote for the *Globe Democrat*, I was not surprised at his eagerness to talk and joke with me. Lane had served a term as a Congressman from Indiana and was hoping to return to Washington to represent Kansas when it was admitted to the Union. He was accompanied by Oscar Moseby, a grain factor, and a farmer known as Big Ears King, who seemed to play the clown for Lane.

"We need to clear the Border Ruffians out of eastern Kansas," Lane said, "and encourage the Southern sympathizers to leave by liberating any slaves they have . . . and maybe their cattle as well." He laughed and Big Ears joined in. When I asked him about the free-state constitution which the territorial government would not put forward in Congress, Lane suggested that he could move statehood forward through his Washington friends and support from the Republican Party. "I know how to grease the wheels of government," he said self-confidently. He had a full poke of stories and witticisms, most of them obscene, and I came to believe he saw me as someone who might have influence beyond the borders of Kansas and possibly a political ally.

"Before we can achieve statehood, us Kansans must rid our Territory of Missourians. Robinson is an old woman. You have seen that he won't fight, I'm sure. I offered to break him out of Lecompton but he sits there like a chicken on a nest—rubbing his own eggs." He gave me a lewd wink. "Now I intend to stuff a corncob so far up the ass of the Ruffians. . ." King's raucous laughter erupted, and Lane stopped momentarily. "Well, Governor Shannon's arm won't be long enough to pull that Goddamn corncob out, Mr. Middleton."

Jim Lane had put new fire under the free-state cause. He began calling his militia the "Army of the North," a name, however exaggerated, that encouraged his followers and allies to undertake an attack on Franklin, four miles from Lawrence, and an assembly point for the Border Ruffians. I observed that Lane, curiously, did not lead the raid of about eighty free-soil volunteers, who routed the proslavery defenders and captured one of the cannons that had battered the Free State Hotel in May. Two days later, a larger guerrilla band under John Brown overwhelmed a proslavery stockade at Washington Creek and captured Colonel Henry Titus, a notorious Southern leader. Federal troopers protecting the territorial capital, Lecompton, a mile away, did not intervene. Brown's victorious militia, like a triumphant Legion entering Rome, carried the wounded Titus and some of his men back to Lawrence, the town they had bragged they would destroy. Brown was said to have shown kindness to captured Southerners and prayed with the dying. The next day Governor Shannon and Major Sedgwick traveled to Lawrence for a prisoner exchange. No sooner was that done than on the day following, Wilson Shannon suddenly resigned his position and prepared to leave the state he could not govern. I was sending Downing accounts as quickly as I could write them and get them to the telegraph in Kansas City.

Fortune's wheel continued to spin as wildly as a gambling device. In late August a call to arms in Missouri produced a military assemblage at Little Santa Fe, a town on the state line about twenty miles south of Kansas City. A motley force of several hundred men moved toward the Marais des Cygnes River and on August 30 burned to the ground the Brown stronghold of Osawatomie, murdering young Frederick Brown, I was told, as he walked peaceably down the road. John Brown was said to have fought fearlessly before they destroyed his town. The whole countryside was full of guerrilla bands, and columns of smoke from burning houses and crops rose in the summer air as regularly as the sun's morning ascent into the heavens.

In Leavenworth, proslavery citizens rioted and burned houses of free-state neighbors. I hoped that Downing's man in Leavenworth was providing accurate information since I was twenty miles away in Lecompton. I mistrusted many of the reports I heard. Newspaper headlines screamed: CIVIL WAR AND REBELLION! WOMEN AND CHILDREN FLEE FOR THEIR LIVES! BUTCHERY!! BRUTAL MASSACRE!! Truth, I feared, had become another victim of the civil conflict.

On rare occasions, the Federal forces were able to prevent bloodshed. In early September I followed Jim Lane's force of six hundred men to Lecompton where his intention was twofold: freeing the free-state prisoners and destroying the capital of the territorial government where the proslavery constitution had been crafted. When the U.S. Army under Lt. Col. Phillip St. George Cooke confronted the free-staters, Lane, fearing arrest, sneaked back into the ranks, leaving Sam Walker to dicker with the Colonel. When the militia agreed to disperse, Cooke promised to release the free-state prisoners and Lane's force marched back to Lawrence without a drop of blood being shed. About a week later the new territorial governor, John W. Geary arrived, and the Lecompton prisoners were freed.

As Lawrence celebrated their release, on September 14th a Border Ruffian army of about 3,000 men besieged the town. This Missouri army presented the direst threat to Lawrence yet, coming up from Franklin intending to destroy the town they had sacked in May. Old Osawatomie Brown and Sam Walker led the defenders—about 300, including women and children with pitchforks and clubs—who took positions behind the breast-works and in circular forts erected during the Wakarusa War. I was no longer an observer, but stiff with fear, hiding in the corn fields with the militia, armed with a shotgun and my revolver, the Sharps rifles having been given to the best shots like Dan Cornish, whose voice betrayed his Boston birth. His manner had a calming effect on me.

"You ever shot a man before, Ezra?" he whispered, lying in the dried cornstalks beside me.

"Never shot anything bigger than a rabbit," I whispered in reply.

"Men are easier to hit," added Cornish. "Bigger, for one thing. But don't shoot too soon and waste your ammunition. Wait 'til they get close."

And wait we did—for many hours. Although more free-state men with rifles joined us, we were still outnumbered, and pro-slavery Sheriff Jones had now joined the Border Ruffians surrounding Lawrence. Then late in the day, a boy ran up to the fifty or so of us guarding the west side of town under Mount Oread. "Governor Geary made a truce with the Ruffians. Won't be no war!" Cornish and I looked at each other and took a deep breath as we got to our feet.

"Didn't feel much like dying today anyway," he joked as he wiped his forehead with his red bandanna. Then we ran to a vantage point where we could watch the invading army prepare to depart and the Federals under Cooke drawn up before the town: altogether five or six thousand men who would live an-other day. The proslavery army was a fearful sight with their black flags flying, cannons and carriages decorated with black emblems of death. Governor Geary had demanded they return to Missouri and they had complied. In his first days in office, he had prevented the destruction of Lawrence and the slaughter of its inhabitants.

During Bleeding Kansas—the summer of 1856—scores of combatants and innocent civilians were killed in the Kaw and Wakarusa Valleys, log forts, houses, and barns were destroyed, and crops burned in the fields. Two versions of a Kansas Constitution—the Lecompton and the Topeka—were mired in Congress, and proslavery Southern sympathizers still controlled the territorial government. Statehood and peace were farther away than ever, and now without intending to, I had become a participant in the struggle.

CHAPTER FIVE

By ending the turmoil in eastern Kansas, Governor Geary seemed to have done the impossible, but he did not address the underlying causes of the conflict. Perhaps the actual reason for the temporary peace, as some cynics suggested, was simply that the combatants were weary of the burning and killing, or possibly the quiet came from the departure of Old Osawatomie Brown, who had left Kansas to raise funds in the East.

By the end of September, the evenings began to cool down, the days clear and still warm. West of the town's center—the blackened skeleton of the Free State Hotel—cornstalks stood in the fields where I had crouched with Henry Sonnet's old shotgun and Dan Cornish, waiting for the invading Missouri bushwhackers and a battle to the death that never occurred. The dried leaves on the stalks hung like strips of parchment around the heavy heads of corn. Leona's onions, carrots, and potatoes had been dug and stored in the root cellar, misshapen vegetables thrown to the pigs. Only squash and pumpkins on their withering vines remained in her garden. Oaks and maples in the hills started to turn color and scarlet to appear on the tips of the sumac at the edge of town.

I followed the presidential campaign through the *Globe Democrat*, issues of which Downing regularly sent in the mail. He was certain that John C. Fremont, the Republican candidate who promised to keep slavery out of the Territories, would garner few votes in the South and thus had no chance of winning the presidency. So, for me, the election in November held little suspense and would offer no relief for Kansas.

Freed from Lecompton Gaol, Charles Robinson continued to build his extralegal free-state administration while James Lane worked to train his private army and thwart the "governor" at every turn. I continued to think of them as Shakespearean opposites, the idealist and the demagogue—Robinson, a man of honor like Brutus, Jim Lane the Machiavellian, crowd-pleasing Antony—but I was sobered by the knowledge that it was the paltering Antony who triumphed. Except for Governor Geary, they were probably the two most powerful men in the Territory. Geary, a tall, handsome man who served in the Mexican War, was the third of the territorial governors, the first who was both competent and even-handed; in fact, Henry thought he showed sympathy for the antislavery party, despite serving a President who did not. Robinson's return to Lawrence pleased me because he discouraged violence, despite the difficulty in controlling Lane, who continued to harass proslavery settlers when he could avoid the overextended U.S. Cavalry.

To no one's surprise the Republican candidate, Fremont, running principally on the Kansas question, lost to James Buchanan; the Democrats carried some of the northern states and all the southern ones, who expected Buchanan to continue to protect the rights of slave owners. Except in the North, it had been an election in which popular sovereignty swept away the opposition.

Then early the next year, before Buchanan was sworn in, the Supreme Court announced a decision in the Dred Scott matter that dealt a terrible blow to abolitionism, ruling, in effect, that Negro slaves were and always would be the property of their slave masters, even if they escaped to a state where slavery was forbidden. Now it was imperative for fleeing slaves to be transported on the Underground Railroad, not just to free states like Illinois and Iowa but across the border into Canada. Even a state constitution would not protect from the bounty hunters or U.S. marshals with court orders the hundreds of escaped slaves in Kansas—including those living in shanties along the wooded banks of the Kansas River.

With the Territory quiet after the election, I decided to return to St. Louis for Christmas, so I booked passage on the river packet to that city. Missouri militiamen still searched the boats for abolitionists and New Englanders, but I was traveling down-river and, in any case, didn't have a Yankee accent so my journey was uneventful. After an absence of six months, I was welcomed warmly by my father and two brothers: Ira Augustus and Elijah Plutarch. I am, of course, Ezra Pliny Middleton, so named by a Rome-loving father. Now Elijah's wife, Emerald, was carrying the next Middleton.

Russell Downing seemed pleased to see me, hugging me like a family member, and immediately asking about Kansas. He said my descriptions of Jim Lane had sold many newspapers, laughed, and reminded me to stay close to Lane, his hound dog at heel. The rest of the country was also fascinated by Old Osawatomie Brown and there was much speculation in the press of his whereabouts. For a newsman several hundred miles away, Downing had a good grasp of Kansas questions, to which in part I immodestly credited my full reports to him. He also filled my head with suggestions about other fish he wanted hooked in the Territory's turbulent and murky waters.

Christmastime was festive: dinners, balls, concerts, plays, old friends and new acquaintances. I imagined Leona in Lawrence feeding animals on snowy mornings, Henry riding in his wagon behind straining mules, his stable boy, Isaac, bringing wood into the house for the fireplace, and the townspeople trekking down the frozen mud of Massachusetts Street.

At the end of my holiday, these images, however, were wiped from my mind at a ball when I met one Hannah Waterhouse, a pale young woman of about eighteen years. Although I tried to exhibit my best Eastern literary upbringing, she seemed to regard me as she might a savage Kansas Indian, and I soon realized that in trying to impress her I had only ended up playing the fool, the bumpkin.

"One wonders whether there are balls in Kansas Territory, Mr. Middleton," she observed, suggesting the territory's name a word too coarse to be spoken in genteel company. "Are the manners there not rustic?"

She was handsome enough, her wavy hair—drawn back from her face—a rosy copper that shimmered under the gaslight. She was tall, with a slim waist and an ample bosom filling a green satin ball gown, but she seemed to possess a contemptuous spirit as exhibited in her proud and scornful expressions.

"So, who are *you*, Miss Waterhouse?" I asked with a touch of sarcasm in my voice.

Without looking me in the face, she said almost in a whisper "A maiden never bold. . ."

"Like Desdemona?" I responded, recognizing her line. Her icy condescension had melted away. I felt a shortness of breath as a thrill raced through my body. "And with a voice ever soft, gentle, and low . . . like Cordelia?"

"Like Cordelia, yes," she said, now looking me defiantly in the face, as though offering a challenge. "And will you not tell me who *you* are?" She was speaking a line from *Much Ado*, I thought—the masquerade scene where Beatrice questions the disguised Benedick. I have a particular fondness for the clever and spirited Beatrice.

"The Prince's jester, a very dull fool," I replied, quoting Beatrice's description of Benedick. "So, you must be. . .?"

"Lady Disdain," she responded laughing. "Beatrice! Lady Disdain. You know the Bard's heroines, Mr. Middleton," she said, searching my face. "Why *is* that?"

"Because they are the clever and wise ones, Miss Waterhouse," I said, suddenly feeling an excitement I had never experienced in my life. "They teach the men in the comedies what true love is—never fickle but selfless and patient." Feeling my face blush crimson, I smiled broadly—and foolishly too, I suppose. Still, I knew what I was feeling was no dishonest passion but intense impulses of the most tender kind. Or so I told myself.

"Certainly, but it is the women in the comedies who are the most determined, the most importunate, is that not so? Perhaps the wisest characters, after the Fools. Do you not agree?"

"Yes, yes," I agreed, but returned to her earlier question. "At home, I learned more about the plays than I did at school. We read the plays and discussed them at dinner most nights. My father loved Shakespeare and taught me to love him too. I know many lines by heart."

"I attended a girls' seminary. I *did* learn about them at school and played roles in some of them."

"And did you play Beatrice?" I asked. She smiled for the first time—a flash of sunlight—and nodded. One line from Shakespeare wheeled through my mind like a runaway buggy. I snatched at it but did not voice it: *Even so quickly may one catch the plague?* This sentiment in Olivia's soliloquy in *Twelfth Night* occurs at the moment she realizes she has fallen in love, although, comically, she is enamored of another woman disguised as a man.

"Which character do you favor, Mr. Middleton?" she asked. Her eyes sparkled and the faint freckles across her cheekbones gave her a color that bonneted ladies, kept from the sun, could never possess. I could feel my passion rise within me.

"Well, perhaps Rosalind," I said slowly, trying to draw out my response so that our conversation would not end. "She pairs off the characters when they are lost in the forest of their own feelings."

"Lost in their own Forest of Arden," Hannah replied, nodding slightly but still smiling. But *which* is your favorite comedy then? I must be precise in my questions with you, I see."

I laughed and continued to hold her gaze. "It's *Twelfth Night*. So many people so desperately in love . . . until Fortune in one scene effects a resolution of pure happiness for everyone."

"Except for poor Malvolio," she said softly. "Poor rejected Malvolio."

"Yes," I said. "Except for Malvolio."

"And shall we correspond about the Bard?" Hannah asked, looking at her family, who were preparing to leave the ballroom, and touched my arm. "Until you return." I shall never forget that phrase.

On my journey up the Missouri, I thought of Hannah both day and night. She was bold, bold as Beatrice—and like Desdemona too, for that matter, who defies her father to marry the black Othello. To the boldness could be added all the other virtues Benedick discovers in his quarrelsome dancing partner. Witness his soliloquies in the Second Act. I put a letter in the post from Jefferson City and another from Kansas City. I wondered if she would marry me if Downing could find me a job in St. Louis, if my father would take me into his firm, if she would wait for me, if she would follow me to Kansas. All these questions could be asked in the letters I intended to write in the winter and the spring.

James Buchanan was inaugurated in early March of 1857, but no one thought the Federal policy in Kansas would change for the better. When Sheriff Sam Jones, who had led every bushwhacker attack on Lawrence, resigned, Governor Geary, refused to validate his chosen successor, William Sherrard, a violent slavery proponent. Sherrard then threatened the governor and apparently laid a plot to assassinate him. In an argument in the Lecompton legislative hall, Sherrard and antislavery opponents exchanged gunfire and Sherrard was shot in the head and died. John Geary, frustrated and fearing for his life, had had enough and slipped out of Kansas, never to return.

He had, however, provided a few months of relative calm, allowing the people of Lawrence to replace many of the log houses on Massachusetts Street with frame, brick, or stone buildings and convincing Shalor Eldridge to pull down the ruins of the Free State Hotel and begin to replace it with a new stone structure to be called the Eldridge House. In May free-soil pilgrims in covered wagons began to arrive in the Territory, now coming down Lane's trail through Nebraska more often than up the Missouri River.

Later in the month the new territorial governor—selected by the new president, Buchanan—arrived; he was Robert J. Walker, a tiny man five feet tall and weighing one hundred pounds, determined to bring order and representative government to the Territory. The Lecompton convention, heavily proslavery, returned to work on a document that could be submitted to the voters of Kansas, as Walker had promised would be done, and, after boycotting elections because of fraud and intimidation, the free-state party agreed to participate in the contest for the territorial legislature in October. Because Walker called out U.S. troops to guard the polling places, the election was quiet and, despite some voting irregularities from proslavery fraudsters, fair. In the final tabulations, the free-staters had won a majority in both houses of the legislature, making the extralegal Topeka government irrelevant. Blaming President

Buchanan for the failure of the territorial government to resolve the constitutional impasse, Walker resigned in anger. I had spent the summer of 1857 riding back and forth to Lecompton while continuing to watch Lane, who gave rabblerousing, incendiary speeches but took no action that threatened the peace.

Each of my peregrinations around the Territory ended with a return to Lawrence, where letters from Hannah awaited me. Of course, Henry was greatly amused at the number of letters he carried back and forth to Kansas City; he joked that travel on the Missouri had slowed by a day owing to the heavier mail, and that his mules had worn their legs down to the fetlock. Leona, on the other hand, had become my confidante. Occasionally, I read parts of Hannah's letters aloud to her, causing her to blush at Hannah's boldness. Leona marveled that in our only meeting I had not noted the color of Hannah's eyes.

CHAPTER SIX

Since the Kansas frontier was quiet during the winter of 1857, I reckoned it was time to try my wings and fly farther from the nest by penning a story for a national magazine with its Eastern audience. When Russell Downing gave his blessing, I began an account about Lawrence as a stronghold of both the free-state and abolitionist causes. I also continued to peck around Jim Lane's barnyard to supply tidbits as Downing had asked of me and to inquire about Captain Brown. I sent Downing a report on the Underground Railroad since I believed Brown's old conductors were still sending escaped or kidnapped Negroes north toward Canada and safety.

During the winter my mind was filled with thoughts about the woman I had conversed with for ten minutes at Christmas. On Saint Valentine's Day I received a card from Hannah—surely Henry and Leona, guessing the contents of the thick envelope, had withheld it until the fourteenth of the month. With the card was a daguerreotype of Hannah, her hair drawn back, a proud and stern look on her beautiful face with, perhaps, a hint of a smile. In a letter, she exclaimed that her married sister was scandalized that a young woman, not betrothed, would send a photographic image to a man she had only met briefly, leaving me to suppose that Hannah's parents knew nothing of her action. That same day I stopped at the studio on Massachusetts Street for a tintype of myself, barbered and dressed in my best clothes; I asked that it be hand-tinted for good measure. I must have smiled thinking of the consternation that would grip the Waterhouse family if Hannah chose to show the image of her unknown admirer on the prairie.

At the end of the summer, I was again calling at Charles Robinson's home on Massachusetts near the ferry that crossed the Kansas River. In Washington, Kansas statehood was still tangled in a web of politics, with the Democrats trying to hold together a fractured party, the slavery question more contentious than ever, and actors like Senator Stephen A. Douglas of Illinois seeking bigger roles to play. Since Dr. Robinson needed the forum of print to influence votes in Congress, he was as happy to speak to me as when he was confined in Lecompton by the territorial government. After being served tea by his wife Sara, Robinson and I talked politics. So self-effacing was he, that I had to remind myself of his courage when the first two companies of the New England Emigrant Aid Society arrived in Lawrence; then Robinson had faced down armed Missouri claim-jumpers and organized a town militia to protect the small colony. Although he had the bearing of a balding pedagogue, I knew he had a backbone of steel. And like John Brown, he had a mission.

"When we talked in Lecompton a year ago, you spoke of a sense of purpose," I said. "The phrase you used then impressed me—building a New Jerusalem here in Kansas."

"You have a good memory and a keen mind, Mr. Middleton," he said, smiling. "Yes, I see Kansas as the New Jerusalem. My hope is that if our free-state government succeeds here and if slavery can be kept out of the other territories, it will wither away on its own. But let me play the pessimist and employ a different figure of speech: I see the Union now as a divided house and as such, it may not survive." He lifted the china cup to his lips and sipped his tea.

"I am a reader of Shakespeare, sir," I replied, and he nodded. "In his *Richard II,* the King's cousin, Bolingbroke, seizes the throne from the King. A churchman warns against the act, using a phrase from the Gospels: *A House divided against itself cannot stand.* He speaks of England—but the warning is equally true of our Republic, a divided house, half slave and half free."

"Yes, of course. Nevertheless, in the struggle between freedom and injustice, I believe the Union can be preserved by strengthening the cause of right," Robinson said, his voice rising. "Now we see our free-state population increasing, and in many places, proslavery settlers returning to Missouri or Arkansas. And this past spring for the first time, our fields were safe to work, crops

were planted, and the harvest is about to begin—our first peaceful one. Our cause is in the ascendant, Mr. Middleton."

"But the threat of war between the slave states and those that
opposed slavery continues. So, what instructions do you give
your followers?" I asked.

"Defend yourselves against the Border Ruffians, of course,"
he responded, gesturing to me. "But do not lift a finger against
Federal authority. Ours is a moral cause and the country
watches us. We control the territorial legislature now—both
houses—but the governor answers to a proslavery president,
Buchanan. We must still be vigilant." He stopped and laughed.
"You know all this, of course, Mr. Middleton. You have told the
country about Kansas in your paper. Forgive me."

"I hope I can write about a peaceful Kansas this autumn and
a constitution," I said, rising and shaking his hand. Yet as I
walked away from his house, I wondered if perhaps John Brown
was correct: that slavery would only be eradicated by force.

That evening Henry Sonnet was jubilant over his acquisition
of a larger freight wagon to haul lumber and window glass for
the ironmonger on Massachusetts; with the wagon came a
driver, Black Bob Mooney, who was not a Negro but a white man
with thick ebony hair and eyebrows like furry caterpillars. After
dinner, Henry brought out his pipe and his banjo and Leona
and I sat in the light of the kerosene lamp while he played, and
we sang. Several days before, I had received a humorous letter
from my father which I had saved for just such a night of merriment.

Before I left St. Louis at Christmastime, I had asked my father for the address of the Waterhouse family so I could write to
Hannah. Her father, George Waterhouse, a banker well known
to my father for his wit and wealth, had invited my father to dinner. His daughter, he said, was a notorious scold who mocked
and ridiculed all her suitors, and he was prepared to offer a
handsome dowry if someone—anyone—would take her off his
hands. My father laughingly wondered if I were indeed looking to
marry such a shrew. Henry guffawed; Leona, to whom I had
read many of Hannah's tender sentiments was outraged by her
father's comments. When I assured them that I intended to ask

for her hand when I returned to St. Louis at Christmas, Henry pulled from hiding a bottle of fine brandy and we toasted my wife-to-be amid much laughter.

The cooler weather which announced the end of summer also brought the golden sunlight of autumn. The harvest had been bountiful, the countryside now rich browns and yellows, with each day bringing my departure for St. Louis closer. At the beginning of October, I was informed by *Harper's New Monthly Magazine* that my story about Lawrence would appear in the November issue. In it I described the landscape—the steep slope of Mount Oread, the low peaks of Blue Mound to the southeast, the Kansas or Kaw River—and the people—Charles Robinson and John Brown and Jim Lane—as well as the hardships faced by the townspeople of Lawrence and the farmers in the Wakarusa Valley. I planned to take a copy to Downing and another to Mr. Waterhouse when I called on his daughter. I also traveled to Leavenworth, the most populous town in the territory to meet Quirk, Downing's man there. It had more dogs than people and more pigs than dogs. In truth, it was a wretched place, catering to all the basest appetites of military men at the nearby fort: whiskey saloons, brothels, gambling dens—Sodom on the Missouri, without question. Quirk seemed happy to be there.

On November fifth, word came that Old John Brown was back in Kansas, stopping at the Whitman farm northwest of Lawrence. It was one of Edmund Whitman's sons who arrived at Sonnet's house to ask me to ride with him to the farmhouse if I wished to see Brown. The morning was cold and frost and powdery snow dusted the ground as we rode in silence under heavy gray clouds.

Captain Brown, dressed in black, looked thinner and older, chiefly, I think, because he now had a long white beard, untrimmed. I thought he might be accompanied by his sons or the Scotsman James Redpath, but instead, I was introduced to three young men named Kagi, Stevens, and Cook, all of them better dressed than their leader, well-mannered, and intelligent.

"I'm pleased to see you again, Mr. Middleton," he said in his reedy voice, offering his hand.

"And a pleasure to see you, Captain," I replied, extending my hand. I was again surprised by the strength of his grip. "I offer my condolences on the loss of your son, Frederick."

"You are kind to remember him. He is with the Lord—in Abraham's Bosom. Finally, at peace." Although the old man sometimes had frayed trouser cuffs, today only shiny spots at each knee marred his pant-legs, perhaps occasioned, I thought, by religious devotion.

"It's cold in here. Put more wood on the fire," Whitman called to the elder of his sons, who threw two logs in the fireplace. After dinner, the women having left the table, we men drew our chairs closer to the fire and Whitman's two sons were allowed to join our company.

"I know the time left to me is brief," Brown said, turning his unblinking gaze on me, or so I thought. "God has called me to free the slaves. We march in the army of God Omnipotent, clad in the armor of righteousness, protected by the shield of truth, and bearing swords of justice to smite the slave masters and strike off the shackles of the enslaved." He stood before us, slightly stooped, but with the fervor of a preacher. "The crimes of this land can only be purged with blood." Although they had surely heard this before, everyone waited in silence for the old man to continue. "I have returned to Kansas to attend to some work here, but I shall soon depart for the East. More men will join us in the coming days." He paused and cleared his throat. "Under God's guidance, we shall now carry the war to Virginia!" Brown's followers grunted, and Whitman and I looked at each other. I knew him to be a committed abolitionist, but he seemed as shocked by the word "war" as I was.

"Not only are the Negro men chained and beaten," the Captain continued," but the women are forced into concubinage. They labor during the day in the field or the plantation house, and at night in the slave master's bed . . . and the offspring—the mulatto offspring—often are sent to the slave market to be sold to a plantation far away!" Brown paused, his raptor eyes watching us, his fists clenched, now out of his chair. "Slavery is an abomination in the eyes of the Creator." For me, he still had the look of an Old Testament prophet—even more so with his long beard—but now his oracle was one of blood and blood.

"We'll give 'em 'Jesse' believe me," said one of the young men, Kagi, I believe it was.

"With respect, I ask this, Captain," I said, "but how is that war to be fought?"

"Not everything can be explained yet," he said calmly. "Of course, you can write whatever you wish, Mr. Middleton. Indeed, I hope you will report what I say for it will strike terror into the guilty hearts of the slave masters. We shall arm the Negroes with firearms and also pikes—pikes with blades affixed like the ones my sons carried at the forts in Lawrence. The Negroes can be trained to use the pikes to fight for their freedom when *we* go to battle with them." His followers nodded in approval and murmured.

His plan was extremely alarming. A slave army would produce unimaginable bloodshed, Negroes with weapons seeking retribution for years of mistreatment and whites, terrified for their families, slaughtering blacks indiscriminately, perhaps with Federal troops by their side in a firestorm of destruction and blood. It was madness, I thought, madness! "We can free a hundred slaves here and kidnap some in Missouri, but Virginia is the prize," he exclaimed. "We can free *thousands* of Negroes there. Our aim is to start a slave rebellion. Once we succeed in Virginia, the movement will spread across the South!"

Later, filled with dismay, I bid Brown and his companion's good-bye, not knowing if I would ever see them again. Although he had been successful in eluding the army in Kansas scrub oak, Federal forces in Virginia was another matter entirely.

"Do you know where he plans to strike in Virginia?" I asked Whitman later as we walked to the barn.

"No," he replied. "And I don't want to know! If he's planning an attack in Virginia, I don't want to know where."

"Nor do I, Ed," I said, leading my horse from the barn and throwing myself into the saddle. "I have come to believe in the abolitionist cause, but must it bring a bloody war between master and slave? The word 'rebellion' scares me. As much as I admire him, I now fear him more." I waved to my friend and was off down the frozen road.

Still, Brown's words needed to be reported to Downing, I thought, as I rode in deepening darkness down the sloping north side of old Hogback Ridge, now Mount Oread, sleet stinging my face.

As I pondered Brown's words, I recalled Robinson's vision of a New Jerusalem on the Kansas plains; Robinson must have taken them from the stirring hymn based on William Blake's poem. I remembered singing them in my college chapel. But to Brown, a man of literal mind, however, such apocalyptic figures—the Sword, the Spear, the Chariot of Fire—were not poetic words but weapons as actual as the broadswords he used in Pottawatomie against the foe. For Captain Brown only principles mattered; nothing else existed. These thoughts stirred conflicting passions within me: sadness, fright, guilt, futility, and others to which I could not give a name. I shivered beneath my coat as my horse picked his way down the icy path into town.

In a month I would be on the boat from Kansas City to St. Louis, where I would be reunited with Hannah, ask for her hand in marriage, dine with my father, meet my new niece, and begin another of the Seven Ages that every man has allotted to him. Old Osawatomie and his mad plan were slipping away into the abyss behind me.

CHAPTER SEVEN

Like a prairie fire exploding through the big bluestem grass in a rising wind, violence suddenly returned to Kansas Territory. A new word was on the lips of everyone in Lawrence: Jayhawkers! Henry Sonnet was eager to provide information about the mythical prairie bird, the Jayhawk, a name borrowing traits from the noisy and aggressive blue jay and the predatory sparrow hawk and used to alarm greenhorns from the East. Some Jayhawkers tried to portray themselves as free-soil guerrillas who freed or kidnapped slaves and stole the property of slaveholders but, in fact, they more often were marauding freebooters—that is, a Kansas version of the Missouri Border Ruffians of '55 and '56.

Of course, a verb also became current—jayhawking—but the verb lost the little ambiguity in the noun, coming simply to mean pillaging, marauding, and stealing. Now, early in 1858, with John Brown gone from Kansas, as the north of the Territory was quiet, violence had arisen in the south as though the Territory were a living organism in which a putrescent boil, lanced and drained, bred another diseased offspring elsewhere in the body.

When I met with Russell Downing at Christmas, he had interrogated me about tensions in the south. Stories I had heard before taking the boat for St. Louis came from Ft. Scott, about eighty miles down the Ft. Scott Road from Lawrence. Downing said he couldn't spare me from northern Kansas, where the territorial legislature with its free-state majority again was attempting to resolve the constitutional stalemate and where a new governor, James W. Denver, had just been appointed, but Quirk in Leavenworth perhaps could be sent south.

Of course, my meetings with the editor of the *Globe Democrat* did not interfere with my courtship of Hannah. On the day of my arrival in St. Louis, my father and I called on George and Muriel

Waterhouse. Hannah's father was jolly, with an ample belly and sharp nose; he could have come from the pages of a Fielding or Smollett novel. Her mother was petite and gracious and from her, the daughter took her looks. When I saw Hannah, I feared that my heart's thumping could be heard by everyone in the room. Hannah, on the other hand, was remote and reserved, but I noticed that her eyes followed me, left, and then returned like iron to a magnet. Anyone who has ever loved passionately will understand how difficult it was to keep from enfolding her in my arms.

"Well, he doesn't look like an Indian," Waterhouse said, roaring with delight. "Perhaps a bit burned by the sun but certainly as handsome a fellow as my daughter said he would be." Hannah gave a weak smile, looked at her father, and returned her gaze to me. "Never known her to be silent for so long," he added with another booming laugh. "She wakes herself at night talking in her sleep. Never quiet."

Before I could enter the conversation, Muriel Waterhouse spoke, looking at me. "My daughter tells me you are an ardent reader of Shakespeare. That is the highest possible compliment to your taste and intelligence. My husband always said Hannah never could endure a suitor, but I knew better. I have seen the love letters come and go for the last year." Her smile was as beautiful as her daughter's. I was trying desperately to think of a witty remark, but my brain was dry and barren.

"Let's give these young folks a minute or two alone together," she said, "while we have a glass of sherry in George's library." When the others had closed the door, Hannah rushed across the room and threw her arms around my neck, pressing her body against mine. She whispered words or perhaps only made sounds in my ear. I confess that my tender feelings were mingled with urgent impulses that flowed through my body.

"A maiden never bold," I was able to utter as she kissed me. Then we laughed together, relishing our first moments of reunion.

"I have prayed nightly for your safe return during the last year. No lady's lap dog can be as cherished as you shall be when we are married," she declared. "And I shall stop talking for weeks at a time in order to kiss you."

"You don't stop talking even to breathe," I replied, and she laughed. "I can't express my joy. No poet could describe my feelings for you."

"Then speak the lines that several times you wrote to me. From *The Winter's Tale*—Florizel's lines to Perdita. So, fitting since I truly was 'the lost one' before we met."

"Yes, of course, I know the lines you mean." I took a breath. "'Each your doing, / So singular in each particular, / Crowns what you are doing in the present deeds, / That all your acts are queens.'" I spoke them slowly, looking at her and was rewarded with her effulgent smile and another kiss.

Before I left St. Louis, I had asked for Hannah's hand in marriage. "What's taken you so long?" Waterhouse asked merrily. All the wedding arrangements were left to Hannah, her mother, and sister, with my betrothed insisting that the nuptials occur as quickly as possible. When I spoke to Downing about my reportorial assignments, he suggested I stay near home and follow the activity of the Jayhawkers on both sides of the state line since some slaveholders remained in far eastern Kansas, and Missouri was also ripe for raiding. In truth, the Jayhawkers seemed not overly particular about whom they pillaged; if a proslavery farmer were not available, a Kansas free-stater would suffice.

Leaving my bride in St. Louis with her parents seemed sensible given the dangers of the frontier, but, like Desdemona, Hannah insisted that she accompany her new husband, and I was easily convinced by the force of her arguments. Our view prevailed: that Hannah would be safe in Lawrence with my friends to safeguard her welfare. Hannah was triumphant.

Our wedding day was set for the second week in April and on returning to Lawrence I announced to Henry and Leona that I was to wed and would bring my wife back with me. In the time before I returned for the wedding, I spoke to everyone who had proven to be a reliable source of information about the Jayhawkers and read newspapers regardless of party or persuasion. Then in early February, I learned from Charles Robinson that Jayhawkers under James Montgomery had attacked and captured the proslavery town of Fort Scott under the noses of the U.S. troopers at the nearby fort. Robinson was irate at this breach of the peace. I hoped that Downing had received a full report from Quirk, whom I supposed was now in Ft. Scott. According to the report, Montgomery, a former Methodist preacher, had announced that he intended to clear slaveholders from southern Kansas. When I departed for St. Louis and the wedding, it seemed that all hope for a quiet summer had gone to smash.

After April rain, the great Missouri River ran full and swifter than normal, but I now understood the country saying "as impatient as a bridegroom" when I stood on deck and watched trees and towns slowly slip by. Then, finally, St. Louis and the wedding and at last all the rites of love. Two days later, boxes, chests, and trunks loaded on the river packet, our families gathered at the quay, we—Hannah and I—began our journey upriver as man and wife.

Hannah was fascinated by the dress, speech, and demeanor of the passengers on the boat, curious about why so many men chewed tobacco (and an occasional woman as well) and why the streets of Kansas City were still mud paths. Of course, we had private accommodations whereas in many hotels men slept four to a bed, sometimes more. She professed to find nutritious the meals of side pork and cornbread and chicory coffee, finding it humorous that pigs filled the streets of Westport.

We spent the night at the Harris House Hotel, where I had stopped two years before, and the next morning was conveyed into Kansas Territory by one of Henry's freight wagons, Hannah's belongings filling the back. The driver, Black Bob, carried a rifle and I now wore a pistol in my waistband. He explained that all was quiet along the California Road, although he was unsure about Fort Scott to the south; still, we needed to be prepared for trouble.

No place on earth can rival Kansas in April: the blue sky opened above us like a ceiling entirely of glass, the tallgrass prairie moving imperceptibly in the breeze, and birds floating so high they seemed suspended from the sun. Despite the traffic—wagons, and horsemen heading west—the prairie was as quiet as a grand cathedral, swallowing the noises of mules and wagon in a holy silence. When we came into Lawrence, people filled the street, waving and cheering for my new wife as they might if a popular politician had ridden into town. Dogs and children caught up in the excitement, ran behind the freight wagon and the lathered mules. Leona, having heard the ruckus, ran outside when we turned off Massachusetts to approach the Sonnet barn and stables. "So, this is home?" Hannah said, not quite putting it as a question. "Ezra, I love it!"

Each of our fathers had given us substantial wedding gifts and I had been paid for a story on Jayhawkers for *The Atlantic Monthly* so before leaving for St. Louis I had asked Henry to look for a house I could purchase. Explaining that with settlers flowing into the territory and demand for housing and land rising sharply, Henry believed I should buy a house before speculators, "jumping like toads under a harrow," recklessly drove up prices; in fact, he had already picked out the house, knew the right price to offer, and what renovations needed to be undertaken. So, within three days, I was ready to go back to work for Downing, Hannah safely housed for a few days with Leona.

On a cool and rainy morning, I set off for the border, first to Little Santa Fe, about five miles south of Westport in Missouri and then to Monticello Township about ten miles southwest of Kansas City, not far from the Indian Mission in Kansas, Shawnee Mission, a circuit that would keep me from home for two or three nights. In Little Santa Fe no depredation had occurred, although several persons spoke of fears that the Kansas troubles would spill over the state line into Missouri.

On the second day, I rode into Monticello and a pleasant surprise: there to welcome me was my friend James Butler Hickok. A head taller than anyone else I knew, Hickok was over six feet, strikingly handsome with sharp features, auburn hair and sandy mustache with trimmed goatee. Graceful for a big man, he was soft spoken and reserved. No longer dressed in a shirt of homespun, he now wore a Prince Albert vest and frock coat and carried two pistols, butts forward in the manner of a pistoleer. He did not stick his guns in the waistband of his trousers as he had done in Lawrence.

"Middleton, the news writer!" Jim called out. "Sure, it is good to see you again. I'm Constable in the township—since March."

"Last time I saw you, you were with General Lane—lieutenant or bodyguard, eh? We drank beer while you talked about Lane's Free State Army."

"Well, now I try to catch horse thieves and do a little farming too," he replied. He looked a bit of a dandy now, not dressed to follow a plow. "You still in Lawrence?"

"I am," I answered, "but I've got a wife now. Married about a month ago."

"Don't that beat all," he burst out and grabbed me by the hand. "Ezra, congratulations!"

"Any jayhawking going on around here?" I asked. "That's what brings me here."

"Not as such, no. Just ordinary horse thieving, which I promised to stop," he answered with a laugh. "Pretty quiet most days. Say, it's almost noon. My gal, Mary, can whip us up some dinner." Without waiting for an answer, he led my horse up the road toward a water trough outside a simple frame house. Standing in the doorway was a beautiful young woman, her shining, coal-black hair the sign she was part Indian.

The three of us enjoyed a pleasant meal. Mary Owen was well-spoken and charming, as intelligent as she was beautiful, and I wondered if Hickok might be planning to marry her. They were about the same age—twenty-one or so, about three or four years younger than me. Mary told me her mother was Shawnee and her father had been adopted into the tribe. I wondered where she had been educated but felt it impolite to ask.

I learned much more about Jim, the strength of his free-state sympathy and involvement with the Underground Railroad. "My grandfather had a hidden false cellar at our house in Homer, Illinois, where we hid slaves and I remember several times when our wagon, filled with runaways, had to outrun bounty hunters who were shooting at us. My father and grandfather hated slavery."

"That how you got involved with General Lane?" I asked.

"Well, here's how I got my place," he replied, stroking his mustache, as I noticed he did with some frequency, obviously proud of it. "Cost $30 to compete in a shooting contest and I knew I could win first prize for marksmanship and be allowed to join." He laughed easily. "I discovered General Lane to be more interested in stealing Missouri cattle and furniture than freeing slaves." Jim Hickok could handle a gun like no one I had ever seen, favoring Colt 1851 Navy revolvers. In a contest in Lawrence, he ten times drew and hit oyster cans thrown in the air, and stories of his prowess with his fists added to his reputation as a fighter.

That evening he spoke of his brother Lorenzo, who had accompanied him to Kansas but had returned to Illinois. Jim seemed equally restless, perhaps needing a life with more adventure than that of a rural constable. I spent the night with him and left early in the morning, disappointed that my journey had produced so little information, but I invited Jim to stay with Hannah and me when he next came to Lawrence and he graciously accepted the invitation.

May had begun as quietly as April ended, but a terrible incident changed everything. The news came from George Washington Brown, editor of the free-state *Lawrence Herald of Freedom,* the newspaper closed by the sack of Lawrence on the day of my first arrival and, by the way, no relation to John Brown and a frequent critic of his. On May 19, a Georgian, Charles Hamilton, led a proslavery band which captured a number of free-staters around the town of Trading Post. A few were released but eleven were marched into a ravine near the Marais des Cygnes River to be executed. Only five died—the *Herald of Freedom* providing gruesome details of one man spitting out the bullet that severed his tongue and another having his body ripped open by a shotgun blast. Even proslavery papers condemned the attack, and Montgomery used the massacre to attack anyone associated with the Southern cause. I assumed that Quirk, much closer to Trading Post than I, was reporting the details to Downing.

With the relative peace around Lawrence, however, I could attend to my other profession: the law. Owing to my work for the *Globe Democrat* and the political turmoil, I had neglected my legal career, although I had given Henry Sonnet such advice as a growing freight company required. Because I knew that when Kansas became a state and peace finally came to the frontier my job with the paper might end, I needed to establish my legal practice as my father expected me to do.

Nevertheless, I had to continue to monitor the territorial legislature and campaigning for the 1858 congressional election. The temporary quiet after the Marais des Cygnes massacre gave me time to assist Hannah as we moved our household, and Henry and Leona watched over her when I was in Lecompton or Topeka. Then on the 25th of June, I heard the first report of Old John Brown's return to Kansas Territory.

The following day he appeared in Lawrence, accompanied by the Scotsman James Redpath, now a correspondent for the *New York Tribune*, who told me that Captain Brown was on his way to the Marais des Cygnes to join Montgomery. Brown, of course, was not a Jayhawker but as an abolitionist zealot was equally dangerous. When I saw him the previous November, he spoke of carrying his war into Virginia. What had caused the change of plans and how would his presence in Kansas affect the insubstantial peace?

CHAPTER EIGHT

Kansas could only watch as the rest of the country prepared for the congressional elections of 1858, the contest for the Senate in Illinois drawing the most interest. Steven A. Douglas, the incumbent and a Democrat, attacked Republican Abraham Lincoln by charging in a series of well-publicized debates that Republicans were the party of abolition while he continued to defend the discredited doctrine of popular sovereignty. For his part, Lincoln conceded the right of citizens in southern states to own slaves but insisted that Congress could and should limit the extension of slavery into the territories. At the center of the debates was Kansas statehood, where popular sovereignty in five years had produced only internecine conflict and the infringement of the political rights of its citizens.

While the free-staters—many of them now identifying with the new Republican party—followed the political debates, Kansas statehood came to naught in Washington. The Lecompton, pro-slavery constitution, approved by a legislature chosen in an election tainted by massive fraud and voter intimidation; the Topeka constitution written by the extralegal free-state body that had no legal standing; the Leavenworth constitution prohibiting slavery, which was passed by the first free-state legislature in April of 1858; the "English compromise" (named after the Indiana congressman who proposed it): all had been submitted to Congress until finally, the English compromise passed both houses in April. When submitted to Kansas voters in August of 1858, the "compromise," filled with bribes disguised as economic incentives, was derided as "Lecompton junior," an insult to voters, and was soundly defeated by the polls. Statehood now seemed as unattainable as ever, but one thing was clear: Kansas would never be a slave state.

To supply Downing with reaction to the latest statehood de-
bacle, I decided to survey opinion in Lawrence, beginning with a
group that, knowing I was a newsman, usually had avoided
me—the Negroes. Black faces were often seen on the streets of
Lawrence, but Negroes had little social intercourse with whites.
In addition to Henry Sonnet's stable boy, Isaac, I knew Alexander, a barber who, when asked, politely told me he had only one
name; a tailor named Edward Parrish; two cooks whose names I
didn't know; and Tiny Tom Pinckney, a giant muscular blacksmith. Except for Tiny Tom and Alexander, most were reluctant
to speak to me, suggesting that they were runaways who might
claim to have papers but did not. I realized then I did not know
of any colored women, except one light-skinned Negress I believed to be a prostitute.

James Lane continued to blame Charles Robinson for the
death of statehood, although Lane could no more have accepted
"Lecompton junior" than Robinson. Robinson, of course, blamed
President Buchanan, who celebrated a great victory until the
Kansas vote caused him to realize that he had suffered a stun-
ning defeat.

One person who cared not a whit about statehood was Old
Osawatomie, John Brown, and there he was, outside the general
mercantile, having just tied a bag of supplies on his pack horse,
straw hat in hand, mopping his brow in the hot August sun.

"Captain Brown," I said. "Do you remember me? Middleton of
the *Globe Democrat?*"

"Mr. Middleton!" he replied, turning to greet me. "You offered
condolences on my son, Frederick, on a day when I was low. I do
not forget a kindness." Although his beard seemed whiter than
when I last saw him, his eyes were clear as he fixed them on me.
"When I last saw you, there was snow, I think. Yes, at the Whitman farm. Not like today."

"I heard you were back in Kansas."

"Yes, for a time," he responded. "It is needful I continue my
work here." He swung up into the saddle with the agility of a
young man. "I have a long journey ahead of me so you must
pardon me if I leave abruptly." He gave his horse a little kick

with his heels and pulled on the reins of his pack horse. "I am bound for Glory, Mr. Middleton. Bound for Glory!"

He rode south on Massachusetts Street past the old fort from the days of the Wakarusa War, disappearing in the distance, a figure in black, erect in the saddle. In my mind's eye, I saw him, carrying a rifle, running toward the bushwhackers at Black Jack, a younger man, coat flapping, bullets whining through the scrub oak, unafraid because he was protected by Jehovah.

It was no surprise to see James Redpath saunter from a saloon, for the writer followed Brown like a dog, reporting his actions to New York readers. Wearing a collarless shirt and a broad-brimmed slouch hat in the heat of the day, he stepped down from the wooden plank sidewalk connecting building to building to create a promenade so customers could avoid the dung-filled street. His clipped accent was the only indication he was not a man of the frontier. Since Redpath generously shared information, I took him back inside for another drink or two and a chat about the old man.

"He's gone back and forth, Ezra," Redpath explained. "Raiding with Montgomery, then kidnapping Negroes and taking them north, sneaking into Missouri. Been in Kansas since June."

"Then he's given up his plan to start a slave rebellion? Carry the war into Virginia?"

"Far from it," Redpath said, gulping down his whiskey and grimacing. "But he's had to postpone it. Fellow training Brown's troops in the East threatened to reveal the plan and the Secret Six—his abolitionist financiers, supporters—got scared. I know *about* them but not their identities," he said conspiratorially, in a whisper, "but they sent the old man back here for a while." The parlor was almost empty. Three men sat at a table, too listless to pick up the cards that lay before them, while another slept in a chair.

"Is there such a group?" I asked, thinking this the invention of a novelist, especially the whimsical name.

"Oh yes," Redpath responded. "He needs arms and they supply the funds. Many rich abolitionists have waited for a man like Brown."

"This amazes me," I said. "And is the insurrection, skirmish, whatever it was, called off just because one man betrayed the plan?"

"May have been other impediments," Redpath opined. "Perhaps not all the planning was complete. And the Captain's been trying to get Frederick Douglass to join the conspiracy—other prominent Negroes in New York and Canada as well—but they all got cold feet I guess."

"So, he still plans to lead a slave rebellion?" I asked. Redpath rubbed his chin and nodded. Since I was paying the tab, he called for another whiskey.

"Still says he's commissioned by God to free the slaves," the Scotsman said. "Ezra, I don't speculate in the *Tribune* about what men think or might do." He looked at me and took out a kerchief to wipe the back of his neck.

"Nor will I," I replied as we left the saloon. "What you have told me is locked inside me. Count on my discretion." We shook hands, vowing to meet again, and Redpath climbed unsteadily into the saddle, perhaps having over-imbibed, and was off down Massachusetts after the Captain.

Standing in the middle of the baked-mud street as I watched Redpath ride away, I thought of the fortunes of famous men. In the Middle Ages, the Roman goddess *Fortuna* (I had learned in school) became the personification of chance or luck in human affairs, her emblem the revolving wheel. Poets and historians treating the inexplicable in life saw Fortune elevating men to power and riches and then, without reason, casting them down to ruin. The Bard, for example, gives us "strumpet Fortune," "giddy Fortune," "blind Fortune," and many more. Sometimes the goddess Fortune's hands are full, sometimes empty. For John Brown, what lay ahead had yet to be written, but I feared the narrative of this man of destiny to be one of bloodshed and destruction. For Lincoln, a possible presidential candidate in two years, a rising fortune, propitious; even if he were to lose the Illinois Senate contest, he had made himself known across the country, an eloquent orator with a shrewd political mind. Russell Downing liked his stand on slavery: keeping the institution out of the territories while Congress tried to address the political and economic impact of gradually eliminating it, however long that might take. That was my course too.

The alternative was a war that would rip the Republic apart or secession by southern states and perhaps some of the border ones which allowed slavery, like Missouri. The only other possible Republican presidential candidate from the West was James Lane, who had made his reputation as a free-state warrior and fiery orator. It was difficult to see Lane as a conciliatory figure, but he had developed connections in the Republican Party and was raising monies for a presidential campaign. But in a devastating turn of fortune, however, he shot and killed a Lawrence neighbor, Gaius Jenkins, during a dispute over the ownership of land. Although he was acquitted after a two-week trial, Lane's reputation was ruined, and his presidential aspirations shattered. The citizens of Lawrence seemed to agree that Lane's political hopes were dead, but given the capriciousness of Fortune, it seemed foolish to bury the prospects of this contentious Jayhawker so soon.

CHAPTER NINE

Autumn brought the customary seasonal changes, yellow leaves on the trees along the Kaw River and the scarlet of sumac. Corn and wheat and barley were harvested in the fields in and around Lawrence, the grass atop treeless Mt. Oread was dyed a purple-gold, and the days stretched out like a golden cat, satisfied to lie lazily in the burnished light.

When the nation voted in November of 1858, Kansas continued to observe from afar. The Republicans in Illinois polled four thousand more votes than Douglas's party but the distribution of seats in the state legislature favored the Democrats and Douglas accordingly was re-elected to the Senate in a victory over Lincoln. Maintaining in the debates that the Founding Fathers recognized a moral problem with slavery, Lincoln acknowledged its evils and opposed its expansion to the territories while taking care to distance himself from abolitionism and black rights. Nevertheless, on the strength of his performance in the debates, Lincoln, in defeat, increased both his notoriety and prestige, despite the Dred Scott decision by the Supreme Court, which validated the position that owning slaves was a fundamental right not subject to legislative prohibition.

Because the Territory was quiet after the electioneering ended, I could now attend to the activities of my Hannah. On reaching Lawrence, she had planted a kitchen garden, then bought herself a pony (with assistance from Henry Sonnet) and chickens and two pigs and had even learned to shoot; at her insistence, we joined a church. Hannah also helped organize lyceums, lectures, and debates and soon was better known in Lawrence than I, a resident of more than two years. When she and Leona began to teach Sonnet's stable boy, Isaac, and another young Negro to read, I watched with interest. Since both boys proved industrious scholars, Hannah ordered books for their use and bought several for me as well. One was a recent novel I had not read, Harriet Beecher Stowe's *Uncle Tom's Cabin,* which I knew was a sensation across the nation and in Europe. Although it was sentimental and mawkish, I averred that the portraits of both slaves and masters powerfully affected me and caused me to re-examine abolitionism. Hannah and I opined the death of Uncle Tom to be almost as heart-rending as the death of Shakespeare's Cordelia.

When I arrived in Lawrence two years earlier, I felt unequivocal support for the free-state settlers, under attack by the Border Ruffians for attempting to exercise rights promised in the Constitution. Although my father represented slaveholders like every Missouri attorney, my family had never owned slaves; nevertheless, abolitionism held no interest for me.

Watching the federal government deny statehood to the Territory and appease the slave-holding states caused me to wonder whether the cultivation of cotton had not only made slaveholders wealthy and arrogant but contaminated the industrial North by supplying the raw material that made mill owners rich and created the capital for them to expand. A scholar of the art of government might argue that our Republic had become a proslavery oligarchy with corrupted courts, a perverted Congress, and a compliant president.

Because of Quirk's posting to Fort Scott, Russell Downing asked me to set a watch on Leavenworth as well as east-central Kansas. Since I had observed that city to be a licentious place, I found a room in the home of an elderly church lady; there I could spend a night or two each month. Staying true to one's wedding vows poses no difficulty if a marriage is sound, but I lamented the nights I did not share the conjugal bed with Hannah.

Then on Christmas day, Hannah, always full of surprises, gave me a package tied with a crimson ribbon. Inside was a small silver cup and my face must have betrayed puzzlement about the finely-wrought gift.

"My love," she said laughing. "It's for you. To give milk to our baby." With surprise, I looked in my wife's eyes. "It's true! I'm with child!"

"When did you learn?" I asked. The questions came out as I stammered: "Are you all right? Will you return to St. Louis to give birth? Are you certain?" Hannah was radiant as we now shared the secret of new life on the day the Savior was born.

"Such a torrent of questions!" she said joyously. "For two months now—and so the baby should arrive about the first of August. And as to your question about returning to St. Louis for my confinement, I shall write my parents today and tell them as I am a pioneer wife, a prairie wife, my son or daughter shall be born in Kansas."

"But your mother . . .." I began when she interrupted me with kisses.

"Born a Kansan, Ezra. It's the way I wish it," she said. "And if you will allow it, we can return to St. Louis next Christmas with the baby." She smiled. "Our home is here."

Even the pewter gray sky and the cold could not diminish my joy as we walked to the Sonnets' for Christmas dinner, treading on the brown grass to avoid the muddy street, which refused to freeze over. It was our third Christmastime together, I reminded her, even though our first one had lasted a mere ten minutes. The dinner with Henry and Leona became an even more festive celebration when we announced our secret. We were so decorated with smiles and giggles that the happiness in our faces would have betrayed our secret. Leona took us into the kitchen to see the new Oliver cook-stove which Henry had presented as her Christmas gift, ordered from St. Louis and, he informed us, costing thirty dollars. In it, a large goose roasted in its juices, a gift to the nose and the eyes. "Wouldn't you know *my* present would also benefit him," Leona said in mock outrage as Henry chuckled and hugged his wife.

Despite our happiness, we shared our secret with no one else and, owing to the fashions of the day and because Hannah was a tall but thin woman, her condition might not be noticeable for some months. During the days after Christmas, I became protective and solicitous of her, refusing to allow her to carry dishes to the table, feed the pigs and chickens, or ride her pony. Moreover, since I had no experience with women in her condition, when I observed her to be extremely tetchy, I assumed her peevishness to be normal. Thus, I was shocked when she threw a raw chicken across the kitchen and screamed: "You're driving me mad!"

Picking up the chicken, calm but perplexed, I questioned her. "Why *did* you throw that chicken at me, my dear?" I asked.

"Next time, I'll empty a *chamber pot* on your head!" she shouted, rushing from the room. As I considered following her, I heard her in the bedroom, but after a few moments, she reappeared—laughing. "Forgive me, husband," she said. "And forgive me the chamber pot." I walked across the room and embraced her. "I know you seek to protect me, Ezra, but I am not unwell, and you cannot treat me like a piece of china for seven more months." I attempted to explain, to justify, my behavior, but I could see that Hannah and motherhood had already carried the day. She was smiling, but her eyes burned with determination. "You must let me do for myself."

"And so, you shall," I replied, holding her close and wondering when I could feel the new life in her body. Despite my vow and affecting an air of nonchalance, that afternoon I accompanied her to the shops on Massachusetts Street, both of us wrapped in heavy coats against the cold wind. Because the streets were muddy, we took our buggy. Before returning home, we stopped at the bank to deposit a draught from Russell Downing. In his cage sat the bank's cashier, Eli Foster, who greeted us. Eli and I often hunted together, I with the antique shotgun Henry Sonnet gave me when the Border Ruffians threatened Lawrence two years before.

"The next time you and Ezra shoot prairie chickens you must stay for supper, Eli," Hannah said.

"Yes, ma'am," Eli replied with well-polished charm. Hannah thought the handsome Eli had a way with the ladies and expressed surprise he was still unattached. "Ezra," Eli said, lowering his voice, "Osawatomie Brown's back in town. I heard he has a group of runaway slaves he's taking to Canada."

"Where can I find him, Eli?" I asked.

"He was at Eastern House this morning," my friend said as he counted out my money.

"I want you to meet him," I said to Hannah. "It may be our last chance before he goes back East again."

"After Lincoln, he is the person I most desire to know," she declared. "Or possibly Mr. Frederick Douglass," she added smiling coyly.

We hastened to Mrs. Killam's Eastern House, where we found Captain Brown just finishing his noon-time meal. At another table were two of his companions, whom I had met at Ed Whitman's house. The other two tables in the small dining room stood empty.

"Captain Brown," I said, extending my hand. "Forgive me for interrupting your dinner." He tried to rise but settled back into his chair and looked at me with his copper-gray eyes and their unblinking gaze. "I have brought my wife, Hannah, who wishes to make your acquaintance, sir."

Gesturing toward the chair across the table, he spoke with the tenderness he might have shown his own daughter. His long beard, whiter now, made him look even more like an Old Testament prophet. "I have long desired to meet you, sir," she said, speaking softly after she seated herself. "Many have written in opposition to slavery and denounced its manifold evils and the Fugitive Slave Act as well," Hannah said, "but you have acted again and again to transport Negroes to safety in Canada and assisted abolitionists to protect themselves and their rights." Women are, of course, discouraged from speaking on politics in public—and in many families even in private. Thus, Captain Brown seemed at first surprised, then pleased at her forthright exposition, and charmed, I believe, for her views were not expressed in a shrill or offensive manner. Pride swelled within me as she spoke.

"We are persons of like mind, Mrs. Middleton," he replied smiling and drumming his fingers softly on the table. "Our views are in concert."

"I am told you have a large family, Captain," Hannah continued. "You must have made many sacrifices for our cause. Being away so often, do you not miss your family?"

"I think of my wife and family every day and pray for them," the old man said, looking at Hannah as a trace of a smile crossed his face. "Some of my boys are often with me, but my 'family' includes our black brothers and sisters in bondage as well—and I pray for them as fervently. For I say in modesty I am commissioned by God on High to free the slaves, for there can be no justice or peace in this land until slavery is ended. I am bound with them."

"Have you far to go today?" she asked.

"Yes, but the thought of my children goes with me. Their letters sustain me, as do those of my wife," he replied, reaching into the pocket of his black coat and withdrawing a packet of letters, tied with a ribbon. "These comfort me when I am weary— even if I am tempted to follow the road to despair." He coughed and looked at Hannah. "You are young and may be blessed with a child. May every child of your body bring you joy."

Hannah glowed but he could not, of course, have known the reason. For a moment Captain Brown and Hannah gazed at each other in silence. Rising from their table as Brown got to his feet, his two companions gave a slight bow to my wife and me, as the old abolitionist took Hannah's hand in both of his cracked and weathered ones and said: "Now I must be about my work. God bless you." The moment was thrilling, for I was sure he was at last ready to take his holy war to Virginia, where he and many others would surely die. With the departure of the Captain, the room seemed to have had all its vital energy sucked from it, like the vacuum created in a bottle in my college natural philosophy studies.

As we rode home in the buggy, Hannah sat in silence, watching an old Negro woman trying to find sure footing in the mud as she crossed the street. "You have long been silent, Ezra," she observed. "Are you troubled about Captain Brown?"

"I believe he will lead an army of black men and white men into Virginia," I replied. "His goal is to start a slave rebellion. The Army will be called in to aid Virginia. Buchanan will see to it."

"And if it . . . when it fails?" she asked as we pulled up before our barn. She waited for me to help her from the buggy and when she caught my eye, we both laughed at the morning's contretemps. She seemed light as a child as I lifted her down.

"Well, to answer your question . . . John Brown and all his company will be hanged for treason. He was telling us farewell. He knows he will die." Hannah nodded and walked to the house.

CHAPTER TEN

Several weeks later, on a cold February morning, sitting at my desk to prepare information for Downing, I heard a heavy knocking at the door. When Hannah answered the knock, I heard her laughter and a man's voice. Putting down my pen, I rose from my chair to see my wife's head peeking around the corner.

"There's a very tall person here to see you. Quite a handsome one he is," she said with a smile before Jim Hickok also peered around the corner.

"Well, Ezra, I got to take myself to St. Louis and get me a woman like that," he said. Hannah raised her hand to her face in embarrassment, but I could tell the compliment had pleased her.

"Had you written us, we'd have arranged a dance for you, Jim," I replied, shaking his hand. He wore a frock coat, fur hat, and carried a buffalo robe.

"Well, I always fetch my fiddle with me, but I confess my reluctance to write you," he said with downcast eyes, "a news writer of renown. You see, I was forced to leave school early and my spelling's not of the best."

"Nonsense, Jim. Never have a worry about that."

"Perhaps I should write to Hannah, so she could mend my spellings before giving the letter to you." He gave a soft chuckle.

"Put your horse in the barn while I get more wood for the fireplace. Hannah can pour us some coffee."

"I've left Johnson County for good," he said when he returned from the barn. "No adventure in locking up drunks and catching the odd horse thief," he said in answer to my question. "Not to mention the pay." He laughed and stroked his blond mustache. "My brother Lorenzo came out from Illinois in the autumn and went up to Leavenworth and got hired as a teamster for Russell,

Majors, and Waddell. They deliver supplies to the army posts out west. Big freight wagons. Indians and bandits to reckon with, I hear."

"Is there any danger to you?" Hannah inquired with a look of concern.

"No ma'am," he responded, pointing a finger at her as though it were a gun, a gesture I had seen him use before. "I'm a fair shot."

"He's being modest, dear," I interjected. "He can hit an oyster can at fifty yards. Best shot in Jim Lane's militia."

"Lorenzo says I can get hired," he said, smiling at both of us, "and I may be able to stay with the Cody family in Leavenworth. I know the boy, Billy, and his mother rents out rooms. She's a widow. Father was stabbed by slavery sympathizers when he was a youngster."

"Leavenworth's a wicked town, Jim," I warned with humor, "but you're a card player so that's fine." Hannah laughed and Hickok smiled.

"Now don't be talking about all my sins, for I've got a few, I confess," he said, turning to Hannah. "I'm no drunkard, ma'am, and I'm courteous to ladies and kindly to old persons and dogs."

"Of course, you are, Jim," she said. "And Ezra can invite you to spend evenings with his church lady when he's in Leavenworth."

"Better than the grog shops," he replied, "and I can bring my brother too."

Jim Hickok spent the night in our room for guests. I suspect his feet hung over the end of the bed, but probably no bed in the Territory could accommodate such a giant. He left after breakfast the next morning, extracting a promise to visit when I was next in Leavenworth.

As it happened, I went to Leavenworth three times in the spring and twice I saw Hickok, who lived at the Cody house, run by Julia Cody. Her brother, Billy, although only thirteen, was already working for Russell, Majors, and Waddell on the wagon trains as a cavayard, that is, herding the cattle that followed the train. No contrast could have been greater than that between the tall, soft-spoken Hickok and the talkative boy, Billy Cody.

"Known Jim since he saved me from a terrible beating when I was eleven," young Cody said. "Had no father—he'd been stabbed in the back—so Jim gave the bushwhackers the devil." I was confused: was it the bushwhackers who had stabbed him? "Course, I can take care of myself now." Hickok nodded and smiled.

"Billy's a tough one," Hickok replied. "Got to be if you're out on the prairie. Indians, road agents, bandits—and farther west the Mormons, nasty bunch." He was dressed in buckskins now, not the frock coat he wore when he visited us in Lawrence.

The three of us walked to the nearest saloon; in fact, a saloon is always nearby in Leavenworth. Dragoons in uniform seemed to be everywhere and I wondered about the rumor of an expedition to suppress the Mormons, who had been attacking pilgrims on their way west.

"Do you drive freight wagons, Jim?" I asked him as he drank his beer.

"We need long trains to supply the forts," he answered, putting his glass down. "Sometimes twenty-five wagons in a train, each pulled by six yokes of oxen. And the wagon-master's assistants, bull-whackers—about thirty men in all—plus the cavayard driver and the cattle he's moving along at the rear.

"Ordinary bull team can do fifteen miles a day, but I was under Simpson's command when his bulls did twenty-five a day," young Cody added. I had my notebook out, recording details that could make a story. Seeing me writing, Billy leaned toward me and said, "I was with Bill McCarthy west of Fort Kearney on the South Platte—Nebraska Territory—when Indians shot our herders and stampeded the cattle. We followed the banks of the Platte toward the fort as darkness come on, when over the bank above me I saw an Indian—Sioux war-bonnet with a rifle at his shoulder. I fired my old Yaeger muzzle-loader and he fell into the stream—dead. First Indian I killed."

"Pay's good," Hickok said. "And I got the adventure I wanted. Sometimes too much of it."

"The plainsmen are bred by the perils and hard conditions of Western life," Billy mused, sounding like an octogenarian looking back over his life. "I've known Jim since '57 when we walked back to Kansas after our bull-train was burned by Lot Smith, the Mormon raider." I couldn't quite see how this account squared with Billy's earlier one of first meeting Jim. Any reader of Shakespeare will remember Falstaff's comic account of his fight with two thieves who grew to four, then eight, twelve, and finally twenty as he struggled with them. Like Shakespeare's cowardly warrior, perhaps Billy also liked to embellish his stories for effect. Hickok had wandered away in search of a card game, so I served as Billy Cody's audience as I finished my beer.

Seeing I still had my notebook out, Billy supplied me with yet another story—about trapping with a friend named Harrington, breaking his leg two hundred miles from home, and waiting in a snow-covered dugout for twenty-nine days while his friend went for a yoke of oxen and a wagon.

"Sorry, Billy," I told him, "but I've worn my pencil down to a nub. You'll have to tell me again when I've a sharp pencil." So, saying, I went in search of Hickok.

As the months slipped by, Hannah grew in size and loveliness. She would not wear hooped skirts and, because she is thin, she looked alarmingly out of balance, if I may so explain her appearance. As the birthing date approached, I grew more and more concerned, despite Leona's assurance that Hannah was in no danger. Then on the twenty-ninth of July, Hannah began her labor early in the morning and by afternoon was delivered of a baby girl whom we have named Samantha Grace, "Grace" being her grandmother's name. Mother and daughter were healthy, and our house and my life were filled with joy.

In contrast to our good fortune, dire comments on the deteriorating political climate filled the *Globe Democrat* and papers with a national audience. Talk of possible sectarian conflict and secession were now on everyone's lips as the nation seemed ready to follow Kansas into lawlessness and disorder. My every third thought during the summer had been on Old Osawatomie Brown's threat to carry the war against slavery into Virginia, but as the cooler evenings of October brought relief to the parched prairie, I was ready to discount his words.

Late on a Tuesday morning—October 18, it was—Henry Sonnet pounded on our door, holding a copy of the *Daily Times* of

Leavenworth. "ABOLITIONISTS ATTACK HARPERS FERRY!" and NEGRO INSURRECTION!" the headlines screamed. Printed early that day, the paper contained a brief but sensational account of a raid the previous morning on the federal arsenal at Harpers Ferry, Virginia. Through the marvel of the telegraph, that story was now being read in papers across the country and by Downing in St. Louis. Although no names were available, I did not doubt that Brown had begun his slave insurrection. Late the next day, when a copy of the Leavenworth paper was again carried to Lawrence, the outcome of the raid was still in question. The raiders, both black and white, "led by Kansas abolitionist John Brown," were barricaded in the engine house of the arsenal with hostages and under attack by Colonel Robert E. Lee and Federal marines. I could only assume that the plot had failed, the band about to be destroyed, and Brown dead.

For a second day, Lawrence buzzed with rumors and speculation about the raid. Then in the evening, Henry's courier from Kansas City delivered a telegram from Downing with more information on the raid and questions for me about the Captain. Brown was *not* dead but had been captured alive, shot in the side and wounded by a sabre cut on his head. The total number of raiders was given as twenty to twenty-five— including two of Brown's sons—with most of them dead and a few captured. Downing had asked about several of them, including the three young men—Kagi, Stevens, and Cook—whom I had met at the Whitman farm. The insurrection had ended in failure, and, although I could not say whether I was more disappointed than relieved, I knew I felt profound sympathy for Old Osawatomie.

During the next week, more details became available. A stockpile of weapons had been found nearby but no slaves had rushed to join the abolitionist band and use them—not one— and no one knew why. Panic, it seems, had swept the Potomac Valley, but neither abolitionist invasion nor black revolt had occurred. After a five-day trial, Brown and the surviving raiders were found guilty of treason and sentenced to hang.

I could not let go of the old man so easily. Since I suspected my friend James Redpath had followed the Captain to the end, I wrote him in care of the *New York Tribune*, trusting that my letter would reach him. Many voices in the South were raised in outrage against Brown and a few persons in the North also condemned his raid, including some of his old detractors in Lawrence like Sara Robinson and the editor George Washington Brown.

For much of the country, however, John Brown was becoming a symbol of freedom and an abolitionist martyr; Emerson, Thoreau, Stowe, Longfellow, and Whittier defended his Christian and patriotic impulses. On the day of his execution—December 2—church bells were rung across New England and an Anti-Slavery Mass Meeting was held in Lawrence at which a resolution proclaimed that "he had given his life for the liberty of man." I could not attend the meeting since on that day I was in Elwood, Kansas Territory, giving audience to Abraham Lincoln, as yet an unannounced candidate for president, as he spoke on the slavery question. I listened to Mr. Lincoln with a heavy heart.

CHAPTER ELEVEN

With a new baby to hold and pet, the Middleton and Water-house families of St. Louis celebrated a merry Christmas, although the days were damp and raw, without sun or snow. Samantha, five months old, was excited by the lighted candles on the Christmas tree. George Waterhouse devoted as much attention to me as to his daughter or new grandchild, until he pulled me aside and whispered: "How did you ever tame that headstrong girl, Ezra?" I laughed, having learned that some questions are not to be answered.

Despite the festivities, an uninvited guest cast gloom over the holiday: Secession! Awareness of his ghostly presence caused us to leave sentences uncompleted or break off references to the future. On arriving in St. Louis, I had rushed off to speak to Russell Downing, whose customary equanimity had been gobbled up by wolfish melancholy. Virtually all my fears were confirmed by his well-considered observations. Lincoln, he believed, would be nominated by the coalescing Republican Party over John Fremont, the candidate in 1856, now tarred by his previous defeat; moreover, Lincoln, promising to keep slavery out of the territories *could* defeat Stephen Douglas, the Illinois Democrat.

"*Could*," he repeated. "Lincoln needs the North and some Border states—Missouri, Kentucky, Delaware, Maryland," Downing said cautiously. "Of course, Lincoln's not an abolitionist but as president, he wouldn't let the Southerners dominate the government as they do now. That's why the South fears him." I told him I agreed and wondered if voters might be more receptive to black rights this year, if not outright abolition. "Yes, *your* John Brown has seen to that. Many people who never paid attention to William Lloyd Garrison's editorials in *The Liberator* or Frederick Douglass now pay heed to the words of Captain Brown or

Mrs. Stowe." He leaned forward and moved papers on his desk. "Douglas is weaker in the North now that everyone has seen that his doctrine of popular sovereignty has led in Kansas to outright war between the factions." He paused for effect, like an actor readying his next line. "But I ask you, what happens if Lincoln can get enough electoral votes in the North and Border States to win, Ezra?"

I leaned back in my chair and took a breath before I answered. "The South will secede because they don't believe Lincoln when he says he will protect slavery in slave-holding states."

"Aren't those states guilty of treason then?" Downing asked. "Will Lincoln . . . and the Northern states allow any state to secede?" And what will the Border States do—go or stay?" He looked tired as though he had struggled with these questions both during the day and at night.

"Do you think there will be a war?" I asked. The room was still. I could hear Downing breathing, and I thought of him like a judge in a courtroom, waiting to pronounce sentence.

"I do—yes! Think of it, Ezra. Arsenals, forts, tax offices, excise-men, ships in the navy, armories, railroads, and so on and on. Federal resources! The seceding states will want those resources in the South and will try to take them."

"And the Border States? Missouri?" I asked. "What will happen to the *Globe Democrat*—and you—if Missouri secedes."

"Our paper's policy will be to keep Missouri in the Union. I don't much like slavery, Ezra, and I expect you, as a Kansan now, don't either," Downing said, determination in his voice and fire in his eyes, "but I will bite my tongue and *write* that we must protect slavery in Missouri at all costs, just as Lincoln will promise to do. We *have* to preserve the Union."

Before I left his office, Downing and I agreed on some alteration to my duties, regardless of political changes. In addition to following activities in eastern Kansas, I would now keep watch on Kansas City and western Missouri. Later, when I discussed politics and my vocation with my father, he surprised me by urging me to return to St. Louis and enter the legal profession. Concerned about the perilous position of Missouri, surrounded by Iowa, Illinois, and, perhaps soon, Kansas, he was as insistent as Downing that Missouri remain in the Union. I hated to disappoint him by replying that Hannah and I felt we needed to stay in Kansas.

My father accepted my decision to continue as a news correspondent, complimenting me on my writings, but I sensed disappointment that I would not join the family firm and live in St. Louis, which he saw as a shelter in uncertain and turbulent times. Because he looked older and seemed to have less energy than in the past, I spoke to my older brother, Ira, and he confessed that my father had not been well. For the first time in my life, I wondered if I might never again see my father alive.

When we returned to Lawrence in January, I began to send Downing reports on Kansas politics, while vowing to write my father more frequently than I had done in the past. The previous October Kansans had voted to approve the Wyandotte constitution—the product of yet another constitutional convention— which prohibited slavery and gave women the right to vote in school elections, features of constitutions in northwestern states which had been used as models. This bill—carefully watched by Hannah, an advocate for more rights for women—had been tabled in December, again frustrating the territory's hope for statehood and self-government. The booming cannon of celebration along the Kansas River had been cruelly premature.

As I was writing about the disappointment which followed the Senate's postponement of the bill, Sonnet brought mail from Kansas City, containing the long-anticipated reply from James Redpath to the letter I had written after Harpers Ferry. After cordial greetings, he described Harpers Ferry and the engine house at the arsenal where many of the raiders had died. The only two who had survived along with Brown had yet to be executed. Quickly passing over the aftermath of the raid to Brown, Redpath described the trial and his execution.

The old man, still recovering from his wounds, had to be borne into the courtroom, where he listened as his counsel presented the defense. After a brief deliberation, the jury returned a verdict of guilty and, two days later, the judge sentenced Brown to hang. Fearing an attempt to rescue him, Virginia officials

brought more troops into Charlestown as the preparations for
the execution grimly proceeded. On the cold and windy morning
of December second—as Redpath related the tale—military companies marched into position and the prisoner, his white beard
a contrast to his simple black clothing, was driven, sitting on his
own wooden coffin in the back of a freight wagon. At the plat-
form, Brown climbed slowly but fearlessly up the steps and
waited for the noose to be placed over his hooded head. He was
not allowed to speak; only the sheriff stood beside him, waiting
to sever the rope which would release the trapdoor. That being
done with one hatchet stroke, the old man was suddenly
dropped, struggling for a few minutes—five perhaps—his limbs
jerking, before his body became still. One detail from the description stuck in my mind; Brown went to his death wearing
red bedroom slippers.

Redpath concluded the letter as follows: *At this time, I am
writing a book about John Brown of Kansas and his noble sacrifice. Like you, Ezra, I have filled notebooks with events in this
great man's life, events which I have witnessed and must record.
In his last hours, I saw in him the patience and forgiveness of
Christ on Calvary, or perhaps the holiness of an Old Testament
patriarch. If he was mad, as many declared, it was a divine madness. This description might seem profane to those who knew him
only as a man of violence, but that violence, it should be remembered, was forged by the monstrous evil called slavery and
sharpened by the bitter hatreds on the Kansas plains. In the last
months before Harpers Ferry, he would say "I will carry this war
into Africa," meaning, of course, the South, the enslaved African
nation in America. After his execution, I thought his crusade for
the Negro was a failure, but I was wrong. He went to his death
believing he had succeeded in his mission. On the day he died I
cut off a piece of his scaffold, which I revere like a fragment of the
True Cross. It serves to remind me of that noble figure who played
his tragic role in the theatre of valour and who now stands forever in the hall of liberty. Yours faithfully, James Redpath.*

After sitting for some time examining my friend's letter, I
showed it to Hannah, wondering whether the execution of Old
Osawatomie might be the prelude to a bloodier and even more

violent next act. On the street, at Alexander the barber's and Tiny Tom's smithy, in the bank or the general merchandise, men spoke as though reading from a play script, using phrases like "gathering storm," or "the winds of war," saying "were Lincoln to win the presidency," or "if the Republicans control Congress," so that the act itself seemed less important than its consequences, while the women wondered aloud about the effect on their men and boys, the ones who would do the fighting and dying.

Adding to the sense of foreboding was a drought which began the previous summer and continued with scant winter rain and sporadic icy snow, which sounded like sand when blown against the windows. By early April the Wakarusa River had almost gone dry save for a few pools, and the Kaw, as it ran through Lawrence, was a ribbon of gelatinous mud, scarcely a current at all.

Then this Winter of our Discontent, if I may again borrow a phrase from Shakespeare, was brightened, not by spring showers, but by the exciting news of a cross-country messenger service by Russell, Majors, and Waddell called the Pony Express, leaving St. Joseph, Missouri, at the end of the railway line from the East and running across Kansas and Nebraska and the West to Sacramento, California—faster than mail delivery by ships with the trip by mule train over the Isthmus of Panama.

So, I set off for Leavenworth at the end of April and found that the service had begun on Tuesday the third, running over a route of two thousand miles of treeless plains, desert, two high mountain ranges, unpredictable weather, and hundreds of evil persons—murderous outlaws and road agents and savage Indians. Relay stations were established every fifteen miles and a rider covered forty-five miles, exchanging horses at each station, before passing his pouch to the next rider.

Not a second was to be wasted. If a station had been burned or its inhabitants killed, the rider would continue his route to the next station as best he could. The riders were young men and boys, light in weight, and experienced horsemen who knew that they raced against time. Although the first trip had taken ten days, the company was determined to reduce each trip to eight days. Neither Hickok nor Cody was in Leavenworth when I arrived, but I talked with Billy's sister and for my story in the *Globe Democrat* interviewed a few riders who told of many dangers and hardship. Hickok was too large and heavy to ride, but Cody, small, wiry, and combative, must have seemed perfect.

When Billy Cody returned to Leavenworth, I was finishing my two-day visit, eager to get home to Hannah and Samantha. Young Cody had grown and was much huskier than when I last saw him, but he was still full of stories: a trip to Aurora, Colorado, to hunt for gold, travel to Fort Laramie in Wyoming, and the slaying of a bear that attacked his oxen. I tried to write them down, but the chronology seemed confused, so I ended up with disconnected fragments. One story—about my friend Jim Hickok—I was able to get down whole as Billy told it.

"Indians had gotten dangerous on the stage line, robbing a stage, killing two passengers, and wounding the driver, Lem Flowers, and stealing stock from the stations. We decided to organize an expedition into the Indians' country to teach them to leave our stock and men alone," he said. "Our war party composed of stage drivers and stock tenders and others, and Hickok was made captain of our party."

"How many were you, Billy?" I asked.

"Well, about forty," he replied. "Twenty miles out from Sweetwater Bridge, at the head of Horse Creek, we found an Indian trail running toward Powder River. Because the horses were shod, we knew they must be our stolen stock. We trailed them to the Powder, then past Crazy Woman Fork to Clear Creek, where we saw that another party had joined them. We followed the Redskins deep into their own territory 'til we found their camp. Not realizing they were pursued, they hadn't put out scouts or pickets. Since they outnumbered us three to one, Hickok devised a plan to change the odds. At nightfall, after creeping close to their camp, we rode in shooting and yelling, panicking the Indians and stampeding the horses. After the Indians scattered, we rode through again, shooting at anyone who remained." He laughed.

"Any of your boys hurt?" I asked.

"Nary a one," he said. "And we recovered a hundred ponies, most of them ours."

He apologized for not having any Pony Express adventures—
he had been riding for only two weeks in segments close to
home—but promised stories when I next saw him. Since I was
thinking of writing a story about the Pony Express for a national
magazine and Billy was a born raconteur, this promise greatly
pleased me.

When I left Leavenworth, knowing part of my ride would occur in darkness, I took my Colt Dragoon revolver from my saddle
bag and stuck it in my waistband, even though I thought the
roads to be safe, the only jayhawking occurring far away in
southeastern Kansas. In truth, in all my years in Kansas, I had
only twice used the gun, once when a large rattlesnake came at
my horse. As the buffalo began to disappear from the prairies to
the west, the Indians, whose livelihood depended on the vast
herds, were forced into acts of theft and treachery which would
only get worse. To them, the Pony Express was another invasion
of their sacred land while it was a diversion from a grim future
of disunion and war.

As I rode into Lawrence that night under the light of a nearly
full moon, I could see tender crops withering in the dry fields
and deer, so hungry and thirsty they didn't retreat into the
woods, spectral figures like beggars by the road. I knew that
farmers must already be hauling water from the Kaw for their
livestock and that clouds of dirt from Massachusetts Street were
drifting into the stores and nearby homes even when the wind
didn't blow. Our home was a refuge, and I never needed it more
than I did that night with the troubles of our state sitting on my
shoulder like a coal-black turkey vulture.

CHAPTER TWELVE

During the summer and into the autumn of 1860, the men of
Lawrence gathered for the latest news at Alexander's barber
shop—inside, if the choking dust from Massachusetts Street
was intolerable, otherwise on the plank sidewalk—or, on occasion, at Henry Sonnet's stables on New Hampshire Street. Old
men no longer able to work and idlers of all ages composed this
band of whittlers of wood and chewers of tobacco, lamenting the
continuing drought and speculating about politics and the up-
coming election in November. Lincoln, who had defeated William
H. Seward for the Republican nomination, faced a divided Dem-
ocratic party, split by regionalism; the Northern Democrats
nominated Stephen Douglas, Lincoln's old debate opponent,
while the Southern Democrats nominated John C. Breckinridge
of Kentucky, and a new party—the Constitutional Union Party—
nominated John Bell.

When I heard Lincoln speak a year before—on the day John
Brown was executed—I immediately admired him, careful in his
choice of words, cadences from the Bible, and a morality rare in
politicians. He was tall and a little awkward so that you almost
felt sorry for him, possessing a voice that identified him as a
man of the West, but without the rabble-rousing rhetoric of Jim
Lane. When the election outcome arrived by telegraph in Leavenworth, it appeared that Lincoln, based on the popular vote,
would win enough electoral votes in the North to be elected president despite the Republican Party's absence from the ballot in
ten Southern states.

Papers in the South protested that Lincoln's apparent victory
was illegitimate, but Kansans, casting a more practical eye on
events, rejoiced that Republican control of Congress might finally mean the passage of the statehood bill and admission to
the Union.

Two days after Lincoln's election, I was surprised to learn South Carolina had flown the single-star Palmetto flag in Charleston, a harbinger of secession sentiment. With momentous events both anticipated and feared, we could not consider a Christmas trip to St. Louis this year, to allow our families to see our growing daughter, no longer a babe in arms but a lively one-year-old who chattered from the moment she awoke. Samantha had curly hair of fiery red and I loved her with all my heart.

Hannah was an attentive and devoted mother, causing me to wonder how my own mother, a dim and fading memory, had tended to me. Hannah loved the freedom life in Lawrence afforded her: riding her pony up Mount Oread in the mornings and jumping rail fences on her return home, raising her own vegetables, or walking unaccompanied to attend to an ailing mother or new baby. Somehow, she effortlessly squeezed all the duties of motherhood into an already-busy agenda, and our household ran as smoothly as my mother's chiming clock on our mantle.

Since only the hackberry and deep-rooted cottonwoods along the river had held their foliage until Hallowe'en, November had seemed bleak and dreary, but several days of rain changed the general mood in town and no complaints were heard about the muddy streets. Then in late November, icy snow fell one evening and Hannah carried little Samantha outdoors to catch the frozen snow on her tongue; she screamed with glee. A drought of more than a year appeared at last to be over, and some persons, ignoring the threat of war, looked on the rain as an omen of propitious events in 1861.

Grim news, however, came soon after the Electoral College, as expected, elected Abraham Lincoln the sixteenth president of the United States: slowly Southern states, beginning with South Carolina, left the Federal Union and declared their sovereignty as independent nations. Ominously, Alabama, a month before Lincoln's inauguration, called for a meeting of all secessionist states to consider a confederation. Might the sectarian blood spilled in Kansas in the fifties now dye incarnadine the entire body politic?

In January the Kansas Territorial Legislature had convened in Lawrence just before a severe blizzard blew across the prairie. One subject I hoped would be discussed was incentives to bring railroads to Kansas. Missouri was far ahead; already tracks were being laid for two railroads that would cross the state, the Hannibal and St. Joseph in the north, and the Missouri Pacific, which would carry traffic from St. Louis to Kansas City. It was imperative that Kansas also have a railroad strategy. When and how were the Territory and Lawrence to acquire a rail line?

On the evening of January 29, the snowbound Legislature met following supper to discuss transportation. The overland mail route from Atchison in the north had just reopened after being closed for three weeks. I had waded from home through knee-deep snow to hear a discussion which I hoped would involve railroads.

The door burst open and in rushed someone I knew, Daniel Anthony of Leavenworth, who had founded and was printing the first daily paper in Kansas, the *Daily Conservative*. He was covered in snow, looking like St. Nicholas on Christmas Eve, over his shoulder a saddle bag stuffed with newspapers—copies of his paper, which he gave out, shouting, "Kansas is a state! A state in the Union! At last, statehood!" Although I believe I have recorded his words correctly, I cannot sure, so loud and disorderly was the scene. Men yelled and embraced, others waved copies of the paper. Some people ran into the hall as others ran out into the snow. A few fired revolvers in the air. Suddenly bottles and jugs appeared as if by magic.

Within a few minutes, Henry and Leona Sonnet ran into the hall, Henry carrying a bottle of whiskey. Some folks were singing, some shouting, some dancing wild jigs. Anthony had ridden more than thirty miles to bring the news that the lame duck president, Buchanan, had signed the statehood bill that morning.

Henry pushed through the crowd and yelled in my ear: "They've gone to get Old Sacramento from up to Captain Bickerton's farm—if they can get her through the snow!" (Old Sacramento was the prized cannon taken from Lawrence by the Border Ruffians but recaptured later by the free-state militia.)

The noise and confusion made me think of Milton's description of Pandemonium in *Paradise Lost* and so I described it in my story, knowing that Downing would strike it out, shouting, "Too literary, dammit!" Besides, the uproar of the Devils' court did not fit well with the celebrating Kansans, except for those already corned from the whiskey. Within an hour the old cannon had been dragged through the town and positioned in the street where, a match being touched to the vent, it roared, drowning out the pealing church bells. The cannon fired again and again, and with each discharge, people cheered.

The next day, because travel in eastern Kansas was still difficult, the snow-bound Legislature—at least those members who had sobered up—found it convenient to arrange the first state elections. Politicking was not absent from the hall nor was betting on possible nominees. At home, Hannah was pleased that the new state's constitution—the so-called Wyandotte constitution—gave some rights to women. Kansas, at last, was a state in the Union!

If Kansas shone with the fire of patriotic purpose, neighboring Missouri was riven by disagreement. Secession flags began to appear, and the *Globe Democrat* reported that Governor Claiborne Jackson not only rejected Lincoln's call for troops but was secretly planning for Missouri to declare for the Confederacy. When Lincoln was inaugurated on the fourth day of March, four more states left the Union to join the seven states that constituted the provisional rebel government. Four vital Border States, including Missouri, waited, as did I, now often in Kansas City, to observe events in western Missouri as well as watch the telegraph, my link to Washington and St. Louis.

Then word came on the morning of April 12, 1861: Confederate batteries had bombarded Fort Sumter in Charleston Harbor in South Carolina. Thus, began the war that many Southern sympathizers in Missouri were calling the War Between the States and Northerners the Civil War or the War of the Rebellion—by any name, a national tragedy.

In early June, I was informed by Russell Downing that several hundred proslavery men were encamped in St. Louis, ready to seize the federal arsenal there. I already knew that Captain

Nathaniel Lyon, a staunch Unionist, had been ordered to haste from Fort Riley in Kansas to take command of the arsenal. Lyon, however, used guile rather than compulsion to foil Governor Jackson's plans and save the arsenal's munitions by quietly moving them to safety on the Illinois side of the Mississippi before surrounding the secessionist camp and forcing its surrender. I must let historians of the future decide, but I wonder if perhaps Lyon's action had preserved the state of Missouri for the Union.

In the Kansas election of April 1861, as expected, Charles Robinson was chosen the first governor and Jim Lane, resurrected from his political grave, became one of its first senators, provoking jokes about his popping from the earth like an angry gopher, cussing his adversaries. Ever the opportunist and using his friendship with Lincoln, Lane, hearing rumors that the new President might be kidnapped by secessionists, arrived at the White House with about fifty Kansans—calling themselves the Front Guards—to protect the President. After a week, Lincoln thanked them and sent them home.

In Kansas, intense expressions of patriotism were seen across the state, with volunteers answering the call and companies of men recruited, organized into regiments, and armed and outfitted with whatever was available at forts across the state. The leaders filled their units with veterans from the days of territorial conflict with the Border Ruffians, including old Jayhawk raiders like Jim Lane, fundamentalist preacher James Montgomery, and Dr. Charles Jennison, a fiery and ruthless abolitionist who dressed in an ostentatious flair.

Unfortunately, most of the new regiments lacked supplies, shoes, proper arms, and blankets. Doc Jennison called his regiment the Independent Mounted Kansas Jayhawkers, although it was officially known as the First Kansas Cavalry. Because I knew many of the men he had recruited, I asked Sonnet about the regiment. "A skunk ain't going to change his stripe," he averred, spitting tobacco juice, "or his smell either."

Lincoln had allowed Lane to raise troops—the privilege normally of the state's governor—but he was obliged to resign his commission in order to retain the senatorial seat he had long worked for; however, by accepting a commission from the governor of Indiana instead, he could be both a brigadier general *and* a senator. The three regiments he recruited came to be known as "Lane's Brigade," with an announced strategy to pillage on the Missouri border, burning homes and crops, freeing slaves, and punishing anyone with Southern sympathies. And pillage he did, bringing back to Lawrence horses and wagonloads of booty. Sonnet said he witnessed wagons filled with household goods, silk dresses, chairs, and even a piano; the piano Lane kept for himself, the remainder was sold at public auction in Lawrence.

My worst fears were realized: raids back and forth across the border started again, a remembrance of the old days as the bushwhackers from Missouri and the Jayhawkers, many now in the Kansas regiments, acted on unforgotten hatred. Since Jackson County on the south bank of the wide Missouri and Clay County, north of the river, were hotbeds of Secession sentiment, I felt the need to spend more time in Kansas City gathering information for Downing.

Once a week I traveled to Westport, where I stayed overnight in a loft in Sonnet's stables, an arrangement convenient enough once I became accustomed to the sharp tang of urine from the animals below and the straw mattress I slept on. From there I could take a buggy to the telegraph office in Kansas City as well as get quickly to the California Road and home. Although Missouri remained in the Union owing to Federal troops in St. Louis under the command of John Fremont, I believed that at least half the people I talked with favored the Secesh, as Southerners were now being called.

Then news reached Kansas City in July that at the Battle of Bull Run—the first major engagement of the war—Union forces, after fighting well, left the battlefield in disorder, throwing down their weapons and running. This action proved my hopes for a decisive Union victory to have as little substance as a daydream. Two weeks later, Nathaniel Lyon, newly promoted to brigadier general, left St. Louis to pursue Secessionist governor Jackson in southwest Missouri, where he encountered the forces of Confederate General Sterling Price at Wilson's Creek; after a long, bloody battle in which Lyon was killed, the Rebels triumphed. Between Price's army and guerrillas, most of Missouri, except for St. Louis, was controlled by Secessionist forces.

From Kansas City—a town which seemed equally divided between Union and Southern sympathizers—I followed the inconclusive skirmishes between Price's Rebel army and the undisciplined and poorly-trained Lane's Brigade. Short of supplies, Price was forced to retreat to Arkansas, leaving the field to the bushwhackers. Jennison's Jayhawkers—officially entering Federal service as the Seventh Kansas—were also in western Missouri, alienating many of the inhabitants by their plundering and lawless conduct. In my opinion, the principal achievement of the Kansas regiments in the summer of 1861 was the freeing of thousands of slaves, who followed the Jayhawkers, forming a vast ragged army of Negroes, their wagons filled with their meager belongings, old people, and children. Freeing people from enslavement was noble, but I knew that what the Union needed were victories. Little I had seen of the war gave me hope for a quick and conclusive Union victory in the West.

CHAPTER THIRTEEN

While the rival armies in northern Virginia seemed to move like two pugilists sizing up each other and flexing their muscles but not throwing a punch, raids and skirmishing continued in early autumn along the Missouri-Kansas border. In late September of 1861, I received a letter from Jim Hickok, sent to Hannah as he had promised, for her to correct his misspellings, of which there were a number. Since he was a strong Union man with an aversion to slavery, I was not surprised to learn that he had enlisted in the army at Fort Leavenworth as a civilian scout and fought in one of the first battles of the war under General Lyon at Wilson's Creek in August. Modest to a fault, Jim did not recount his part in the bloody battle, but he mentioned that he was now being called "Bill" or "Wild Bill," the latter name given him after he stopped an angry mob from lynching a boy accused of horse-stealing, and one which he wasn't sure he liked.

Jim's mention of Fort Leavenworth reminded me of news accounts of the demise of the Pony Express after just eighteen months of service and of Billy Cody, the tough and loquacious boy who rode the fast horses across the plains. It had been reported for some time that the Central Overland Company was about to complete stringing telegraph lines from Sacramento to St. Louis so that California would be only an electrical impulse away from any city on the East coast, and on October 24 the first message was sent—a technological triumph that would strengthen the effort to preserve the Republic. Perhaps this news would lighten the nation's somber mood at Christmas. That holiday Hannah and I spent in Lawrence, far from our two families in St. Louis. My father insisted in his letters he was keeping well and discouraged us from traveling in Missouri, where guerrillas were growing more dangerous by the day. Still, Hannah and I were saddened that our families could not see

Samantha, our curly-haired darling, who, once she started talking, was never quiet.

At the New Year, Eastern newspapers contained the first en-
couraging stories since Bull Run: General George B. McClellan
had reorganized the defeated Federal army, renaming it the
"Army of the Potomac" and Brigadier General Ulysses S. Grant,
supported by several Union ironclads called "River Turtles,"
moved down the Cumberland River in Tennessee to capture Fort
Henry, then overland to capture Fort Donelson.

These papers called Grant's campaign the "War in the West,"
ignoring the bloody guerrilla war that continued on the Kansas-
Missouri Border. The preceding November Charles Jennison had
led his Jayhawkers, officially the Seventh Kansas, into Missouri,
burning and looting, but in January 1862 they were removed
from that state and forbidden to return. In April Jennison resigned his command, then was reinstated, yet never returned to
the Seventh Kansas. Henry Sonnet said bitterly that Jennison
was the "best recruiter" the Secesh had. Someone—General
Henry Halleck or Secretary of War Edwin Stanton perhaps—finally realized that Doc Jennison's raids were doing more
damage to the Union cause than to the Missouri Rebels.

April brought unimaginable lushness after the winter rains,
wildflowers of every kind and color thick on the ground, and on
every tree new leaves, the hue of fresh spring peas. In this
balmy springtime came the military news the Union had waited
for. At Shiloh in southwestern Tennessee, Grant's forces in a
bitter two-day battle defeated General Albert Johnston's Confederates in the biggest battle of the war and the first major Union
victory. Then later in the month, Admiral David Farragut over-
ran the forts guarding New Orleans and his Federal gunboats
captured the Crescent City and occupied it. The telegrams from
Downing, for the first time since the fall of Fort Sumter, had a
decidedly optimistic tenor.

I believed there might be a story about the Seventh Kansas,
now being called by Missouri Unionists the *worst* regiment in
the Federal army. Readers in Missouri, I opined, might like to
read about the third of the militant Kansas abolitionists, Dr.
Charles Jennison—a less familiar name than that of John

Brown or Jim Lane. Although many regarded Jennison as a zealot for freedom, noble and generous, amiable and loyal, others considered him cruel and devious, an amoral and despicable thief; no one could be neutral about him. I found the Seventh Kansas near Kansas City and after some difficulty was able to interview Colonel Jennison, whom I had met a year before. He wore a high fur hat which made him look taller than he was, in fact, more like a Russian Cossack than a cavalry officer; this impression of oddity was strengthened by his red-topped boots and fringed and ornamented buckskin coat.

Although the standard size of a cavalry regiment was twelve companies, the Seventh Kansas had only ten, despite Jennison's efforts to add two more, and its total size on the muster rolls was 902 officers and men. Despite its reputation for containing thugs and desperadoes, I found the Seventh little different from other regiments. Since I had turned twenty-eight years of age, many of the soldiers seemed no more than young lads, being asked to sacrifice themselves for the Republic, a thought that troubled me since I had not volunteered. Many of the officers of the Seventh I already knew well. Daniel Anthony, the publisher of the Leavenworth *Daily Conservative*—the rider who brought the news of statehood to Lawrence—was one of the most outspoken and contentious abolitionists in Kansas, having killed a rival Leavenworth editor in a political quarrel. Fittingly, he was Jennison's lieutenant colonel, second in command.

In the spring sunshine, the troopers of the Seventh Kansas lay indolently on the ground, some smoking corn-cob pipes. No one seemed eager to fight. Company A was commanded by Levi Utt, whose emphasis on drill might provide the discipline that the regiment lacked. In Company D, I met a young scholar of military history and Shakespeare named Daniel, someone with whom I wished I could chat longer. Many of the cavalrymen were foreign-born, coming from Germany, Ireland, and England, but most hailed from Kansas and nearby states. On the other hand, Company E was composed almost entirely of men from Illinois. Company K was of special interest because it was led by John Brown, Jr., who was not with his father at Harpers Ferry; I had met him after his cruel mistreatment and confinement in

Lecompton gaol. His company, predictably, was abolitionist to a man and rigidly moral. I spoke to him of my admiration and respect for his father and told him about James Redpath's new book, *The Public Life of Captain John Brown,* which I had read. He seemed greatly affected by my words.

Before my time at the military encampment ended, I saw two men I knew from Lane's militia of territorial days—Jeb and Kenny—who spoke of Jim Hickok. At Rock Creek in Nebraska Territory, he quarreled with one Dave McCanles, a bitter enemy who had threatened him. Jeb's version of the incident had Hickok single-handedly killing McCanles and as many as eight members of his gang. Kenny disagreed, telling a far different story: that McCanles was shot in a relay station run for Russell, Majors, and Waddell by a man named Wellman, who owed McCanles money and had been bullied by the bigger man.

Someone killed McCanles, perhaps Hickok, perhaps Wellman. In both versions, Hickok was described as shooting two McCanles henchmen when they came to their leader's defense and Hickok, accused of three murders, was arrested and put on trial. A jury acquitted him, finding justifiable homicide, a common verdict on the frontier if both participants had a fair chance to defend themselves. Both of my interlocutors approved the verdict, even if they disagreed about the details of an incident that was beginning to give my friend an unfortunate reputation as a gunfighter.

In my experience gunfights were usually provoked by one of three things: whiskey, gambling, or women. Hickok liked both cards and women, and according to Kenny, a woman named Sarah Shull was somehow involved. Hickok was a handsome man with his shoulder-length auburn hair, blond mustache, and thin lips often in a half-smile. He wore two Navy revolvers and could draw and fire in the blink of an eye, and he may have been too quick to use them. In any case, three men were dead. Perhaps the incident showed a side of Jim that I preferred to ignore. As I rode back to Lawrence, I wondered about how much to tell Hannah, who idolized him. Since no one seemed to know exactly what had happened, I decided on a brief account, emphasizing that the West was a violent place where one often had to defend one's reputation or political beliefs.

As I stabled my horse, Hannah, hearing our dog bark, ran out to meet me—sobbing as she ran. Seeing her in tears, my first thought was of Samantha. She shook her head in response to my question.

"Oh, Ezra," she said. "Your father has died. Telegram came today." Hannah rarely cried. She loved my father, of course, but she seemed unusually distraught, almost hysterical, as she held on to me and shook with distress. I felt sorrow and guilt roiling like troubled waters inside me, struggling for dominance: I had not seen my father enough in the past six years. When we went inside the house and sat in the parlor, Hannah began a sentence, broke it off, and struggled to get her words out. Hearing her mother, Samantha began to cry too. I gave my daughter a lump of brown sugar to quiet her.

"What is it?" I asked as Hannah continued to weep.

"I planned . . . to tell you," she said, "When you got home." She swallowed and continued, "We're having another child." Then her body was shaken with deep sobs. "And now he'll . . . never see his grandson. I'm certain this baby will be a boy." I held her, trying to comfort her with all the strength of my body, as though she were a child and I the parent.

Before I went to bed, I wrote letters of condolence to my brothers, explaining that it was too dangerous to travel across Missouri and that they should bury our father without me. In Kansas City, businesses and commercial houses reacted to the Border warfare by moving to Leavenworth, where the nearby fort provided protection. The gold reserves of Kansas City's two banks were transferred by boat under heavy guard to the fort. Although still in the Union, Missouri was regarded by many loyalists as in rebellion.

It was not until the morning after I returned that I realized I had not asked Hannah when the baby would enter the world. "Early October," she replied, still somber. "And if it's a boy, I should like to name him after your father—Robert Henley!" She paused and continued. "I wonder if we might wish to call him

Henley. What do you think?" I thought it would be a dazzler of a name. We both laughed and I kissed her.

In addition to the account of the Mounted Jayhawkers for Downing, I was also working on a story for *Harper's New Monthly Magazine* on Negro soldiers, a politically-volatile topic now being discussed in Washington. Freed Negroes presented several problems. When emancipated, could former slaves become citizens? In the Dred Scott decision, the Supreme Court ruled that a slave was not a citizen and not the political equal of whites. Could Negroes volunteer for the army and serve?

At Cooper Union, Jim Lane had said he would like to see every Confederate traitor die by the hand of his own slave. That fear troubled Missourians even more than Jayhawkers. Kansas—Lawrence in particular—had a population of runaway slaves who had fled Missouri. I knew Lane had petitioned Lincoln for permission to recruit blacks and, in fact, had already begun to drill in secret some he was using as laborers or servants. Was Lane moved by ambition, simple pragmatism, or rare enlightenment? Two other former Jayhawkers turned soldier, Jennison and James Montgomery were also rumored to be recruiting Negro soldiers. Despite a reprimand from Secretary of War Stanton, Lane had enrolled escaped slaves and freemen into the First Kansas Colored Volunteers. Although it seemed the right thing to do, before completing my story, I decided that I should wait to see how these men performed in combat and so put my manuscript aside for a time.

With one child and another on the way, Hannah and I required a bigger house—or at the least one more bedroom. Since I had been using our parlor to see the few legal clients who came for advice and services, I needed an office. When the surveyors of Lawrence first laid out the town, the lots were made ample enough to accommodate a house, a barn and pens for the animals, and a large garden. (In the early days most of the trees and bushes had been cleared—the tree beside Henry Sonnet's barn a notable exception.) Thus, we had land to add rooms to the house—another bedroom and an office for me, facing the street with a private entrance. Delighted with my suggestion, Hannah wished to add flowerbeds and trees as well. Because small rural banks sometimes go bankrupt, I allowed some bonds my father had given me to remain in a St. Louis bank. Now I planned to write my brother Ira to redeem them.

In early June of 1862, I continued to watch the Eastern papers for reports of the war and, of course, followed the stories in the *Globe Democrat*. McClellan's Army of the Potomac had penetrated to within seven miles of the Confederate capital of Richmond, but after the Seven Days' Battle was forced to withdraw. Many papers thought the hesitant McClellan could have captured the Confederate capital and ended the war.

By August, Lee's Army of Northern Virginia moved north and met the Army of the Potomac in the Second Battle of Bull Run, on the same ground as the battle thirteen months earlier and with the same results, a Confederate victory. In September, full of confidence but short of supplies, Lee crossed into Maryland and was in position to threaten Washington. Then on the seventeenth, the two huge armies met at Antietam Creek near the town of Sharpsburg in Maryland. The papers described the Battle of Antietam's losses of dead and wounded on each side as in the thousands, carnage unimaginable—the bloodiest battle in our history.

One paper claimed total losses as twenty-five thousand Americans in one day. The North had won the battle but, because of what I saw as McClellan's incompetence, at a terrible cost. After the first year, there had been optimism that the war could still be ended with minimal loss of life but that evanescent hope was lost in the smoke and carnage of Antietam.

Summer had ended but the weather in Kansas and western Missouri continued hot into October. While trying to keep watch on the Kansas regiments, I tried to attend to Hannah, happy as the day of birth approached. Then on the thirteenth of October, she delivered a healthy dark-haired boy, Robert Henley Middleton, and we *did* call him Henley.

Then a week after the baby was born, Alexander, the light-skinned Negro barber who had shaved me on numerous occasions, told me that Jim Lane was sending his First Kansas Colored Volunteers into Missouri. Alexander and the giant blacksmith, Tiny Tom Pinckney, so black the hue of his skin was almost blue, were both soldiers in the Volunteers, and I had jested with Tiny Tom that the sight of him armed and in uniform would loosen the bowels of a whole Secesh regiment.

"Going to skin us some huckleberries in Bates County, Mister Ezra," Alexander said. "We ready to fight!"

Arrangements were made with Leona for the care of Hannah and the babies, and that night I followed the Colored Volunteers, who by wagon traversed the fifty miles down the Fort Scott Road and across into Missouri. I rode on horseback, carrying my revolver, although I had promised Hannah I would stay away from the fighting.

On October 28—the date was carefully entered in my notebook—the Kansas Volunteers, who engaged a large band of Missouri guerrillas near Butler in Bates County, proved to be courageous fighting men. A week or so before, I had read in a New York paper that a Negro regiment was being recruited in Massachusetts, but since I had seen no report of its use in combat, I believed that Butler was the first action between former slaves and Confederates and the first black casualties in combat—one man killed and several wounded. The Kansas men withdrew in triumph and I rode up the Fort Scott Road, happy with their achievement, to wire the story to Downing. Although the numbers were small compared to those of the massive armies along the Potomac, to me the significance was great: the first Negro soldiers fighting to preserve the Union. Although I have often compared Jim Lane unfavorably to Charles Robinson, today I honored him.

In Lawrence, I continued to get reports about the First Kansas Colored Volunteers. Exactly a month after the fight at Butler, a battalion of Negro soldiers, including some from Lane's volunteers, marched the ten miles across the state line from Fort Scott to Nevada, Missouri, and at the Battle of Island Mound soundly defeated a large force of Southern irregulars and captured their stores. I had given Downing a story for the *Globe Democrat* and now I also had the material to complete my article for *Harper's Magazine.*

CHAPTER FOURTEEN

"The web of our life is of a mingled yarn," an unnamed character in Shakespeare's *All's Well that Ends Well* declares, "good and ill together." Similarly, the moral traits of the men who shaped events in Kansas before and during the war were contradictory yet intermingled, and two such men were Jim Lane and Doc Jennison, both avaricious, ambitious, and bloodthirsty, but at the same time committed to the Union and the manumission of the Negro. In 1861 both had organized volunteer regiments—"Lane's Brigade" and Jennison's Jayhawkers—which not only attacked Secessionist guerrillas in Missouri but, like the Huns of Asia, pillaged, burned, and looted, exacting vengeance on anyone suspected of being disloyal. Old scores from Territorial days were settled with blood and fire.

By early 1862 Jennison's Seventh Kansas, in fact, had been forbidden to enter Missouri, and Kansas was placed under martial law in an attempt to end jayhawking. Jennison's—now commanded by Daniel Anthony—was sent to Fort Riley in central Kansas, far from the border with Missouri. But the damage had already been done: the prosperous counties of western Missouri, stripped of houses and animals, had been turned into an unpeopled wasteland. And after mistreatment by the Jayhawkers, in and out of uniform, some Missouri Unionists had begun to switch sides.

When I came to Kansas in 1856, I was dropped into a pudding of a conflict: the Wakarusa War attempts by the Border Ruffians to destroy Lawrence, the struggles for a constitution and statehood, the election of Lincoln and Secession, and now a war that seemed as endless as the empty prairie. When I won the heart and hand of Hannah and became a husband and then a father, I needed to provide better for my family and so gingerly I entered the legal profession, still promising Downing that I would provide stories and information from the Border. Since the newspapers were filled with accounts of battles in the East, I was now asked to write less about the West, where men killed one another in quiet and deadly obscurity.

Of course, Federal troops were still needed on the border in 1862. Confederate guerrillas—bushwhackers—continued to be active in Kansas, raiding the towns of Aubrey in Johnson County in March, Olathe in September, and Shawnee in October. These raids were led by a man who was no stranger to Kansas, William Clarke Quantrill, and, as it turned out, no stranger to me.

A drawing of the mysterious and feared Quantrill had circulated in town and was recognized by Henry Sonnet as "Charley Hart," a thief and cheat who had come to Lawrence in 1859. I remembered him as a ne'er-do-well who hung out at the ferry on the Kaw. Like the old Border Ruffians, Quantrill burned and looted but he killed unarmed soldiers and civilians as well. According to Henry, Quantrill had joined Sterling Price's Confederates for a battle or two before deserting. "He's a treacherous devil," Henry said. "No conscience. None! Would sell his aged mother!" Kansans had learned to fear the man with the strange name.

Henry and I wondered whether the removal of the Seventh Kansas to Corinth, Mississippi, in late May of 1861 might have been a mistake. Doc Jennison had resigned from the Seventh, according to Henry, because assignment to Mississippi to repair bridges destroyed in the war was an affront to his vanity and thwarted his desire to continue to freewheel on the Kansas border. "Seventh might be in for some hard knocks fighting the Butternuts in the heart of the South," Henry said, stopping to spit tobacco into the road. "Then too, Grant and Sherman are closing in on Vicksburg and by spring the Seventh could be part of Grant's Army of Tennessee. Wonder how the Jayhawkers will like serving under Grant?"

In November the nation took time to vote, and in the elections, the Republicans retained control of both Houses of Congress and Lincoln felt strong enough to sack McClellan, replacing him with Ambrose Burnside, who quickly moved the

Army of the Potomac across the Rappahannock at Fredericksburg to attack Richmond. Unfortunately, winter rains bogged down the Federal army and on December 13, Lee soundly beat the new commander with heavy Union casualties.

As Christmas of 1862 arrived, Lawrence seemed like a safe haven despite the continuing guerrilla war in Missouri. Commander of the District of the Border, General David Hunter had enough troops to challenge the Rebels, particularly after the Kansas Indian Brigade was formed to control depredations in Arkansas and Kansas by Indians supporting the Confederacy.

Hannah and I fondly remembered bygone holidays in St. Louis, even though I felt the hole in my life where my father had been. Nevertheless, my loss seemed less sharp with the passage of time as our children, Samantha, now three, and Henley, two months, continued to knit our little family together. In the evenings with the children in bed, Hannah and I often read aloud from one of Shakespeare's plays, switching roles, which often resulted in her reading lines of male characters, done in a gruff stentorian voice. To be honest, I preferred the comedies, which more often than not, led to carnal displays of affection not found in the script.

At the end of the year, as we were enduring another harsh winter, we received Christmas greetings from Jim Hickok, whose silence had concerned me as we had received no communication for a year. After serving as an army wagon master in Missouri, he explained, he had been a sharpshooter in the Eighth Missouri State Militia before enrolling as a spy for General Samuel Curtis, commander of Federal forces in southern Missouri. "Pretty near all these stories are true," he wrote in telling us how, after posing as a Rebel trooper, he had escaped the pickets of the Confederate army and, under enemy fire, swam a river to the Union lines and safety.

One January morning I was awakened by the barking of our dog, Caesar, who slept in the barn with our livestock. Although the large predators around Lawrence had been exterminated, I had on occasion seen wolves and a panther further from town; now only foxes and wild dogs tried to raid our henhouse at night. Since our pen of rails was staked and double ridered and

our two calves were kept in the barn in the coldest weather, this
alarm came to naught. The greatest threat was the bitter cold:
sometimes the feet of our calves and cow would freeze, the
hooves dropping off when the weather warmed. Our pigs had
been slaughtered in the autumn and cured hams now hung in
our smokehouse.

Hannah, my pioneer wife, stayed busy even in the coldest
weather making soap and candles as well as working at her
loom, weaving linsey cloth for working clothes and trousers. I
enjoyed spending more time at home and less in travel across
the countryside. The *Globe Democrat* increasingly was filled with
war stories from the East.

Despite Burnside's defeat, all of Lawrence joyfully anticipated
a momentous event on the first of January 1863, since President Lincoln had announced the previous September that he
would on that day sign the Emancipation Proclamation, freeing
all slaves in states in rebellion against the Federal authority. Not
all white people liked freeing several million blacks, but most accepted it. I thought it a master stroke by Lincoln and my Negro
friends like Alexander the barber were jubilant. "Can Father
Abraham do that?" he asked me. "Just by saying it? No pass, no
papers?"

"You're *already* free, Alexander," I replied, shaking his hand.
"Every Kansan's a free man, black or white. Besides, you're a
volunteer in the Union army." He smiled the biggest, toothiest
smile I believe I had ever seen.

"I'm mighty proud of that," he answered. Indeed, the First
Kansas Colored Volunteers were now a part of the defense
against the Southern bushwhackers.

As usual, politics were as tangled as a den of rattlers and as
deadly. In 1862, Charles Robinson, the state's first governor,
had been accused in a bond scandal and his old rival U.S. Senator James Lane encouraged the Kansas Legislature to impeach
him, which it dutifully did. Henry believed that Lane's radicals
had vilified Robinson by whispers and innuendo. Although Robinson was quickly acquitted, by the winter of 1863 it was
apparent that Robinson could never regain the trust of the people. Thus Robinson, a man whom I had long admired as a calm

and selfless leader, thought it prudent to resign his position. During the darkest days of threats from the Border Ruffians and imprisonment by the corrupt Territorial government, he had spoken prophetically of Kansas as the New Jerusalem, but now the mantle of state had been torn from him and Lane had triumphed. In the end, the hotheads had brought him down.

As the uncertain promise of spring spread across the prairie, so too did the action of guerrilla bands, led by Quantrill, Bloody Bill Anderson, Cole Younger, and George Todd. I could not guess where any of these bands might strike next. Nor could the Union cavalry. Through June, I followed the action of Kansas regiments as best I could in local newspaper accounts. The Seventh Kansas Volunteer Cavalry—Jennison's Jayhawkers, without Jennison—had been sent to fight in Tennessee and Mississippi. The First Kansas Colored Volunteers scored a decisive victory in battle at Cabin Creek, Kansas, on July second. An independent Negro artillery battery was organized in Leavenworth under Captain H. Ford Douglass, with all black officers; as far as I could determine, the first such unit to see action in the war. The Eastern papers continued to ignore our Negro soldiers and the continuing bloodshed on the western frontier.

Acquiring information about military activity became even more difficult when, in late June, Robert E. Lee's Army of Northern Virginia invaded the North. The Eastern papers seemed in a panic: the Union had earlier suffered a humiliating defeat at Chancellorsville, and General George Meade had replaced Joe Hooker, who had replaced Burnside as commander of the Army of the Potomac.

Now Lee had crossed into Maryland and had entered Pennsylvania, meeting the Union army at a small town called Gettysburg, where several major roads converged. Daily papers in Kansas like the *Conservative* of Leavenworth, which had access to the telegraph, were the best source of current news. The two great armies came together on Wednesday morning, the first of July, and fighting continued during the day. On the second of July, I rode to Leavenworth hoping to get reports either in town or at the nearby fort and, as far as I could tell, after another day of carnage neither army had an advantage. In the afternoon of

the third day, however, after fierce artillery bombardments, Confederate General George Pickett was ordered to charge the Union
lines, resulting in heavy casualties for both armies and a devastating Rebel defeat. The losses in dead and wounded were
staggering, unimaginable, but Lee's invasion had been stopped.

As the Confederate army retreated from Pennsylvania, news
was arriving from Vicksburg, where Grant was struggling to capture the naturally-fortified stronghold on the Mississippi, the
last Rebel territory on the river. On May twenty-third, Grant had
begun a siege of the town and its starving military and civilian
population and, after savage bombardment, on the fourth of
July, the thirty thousand defenders surrendered, giving the Federal forces complete control of the Mississippi—cutting the
Confederacy in half. As I rode back to Lawrence the evening of
our national holiday, I reflected on the two great Union victories
and wondered if, despite the enormity of Lee's defeat at Gettysburg, Vicksburg might prove to be the more significant.

In order to send my report to Downing for the weekly *Globe
Democrat,* I was up early the next day to gather opinions in Lawrence about the Union victories. Along the Kaw, the cottonwoods
and willows wilted under the summer sun and the townspeople
moved slowly in the morning heat and dust of Massachusetts
Street. The second person I talked to was Senator Jim Lane,
home on his Congressional summer recess. I believe he recognized me, but I spoke immediately to identify myself.

"Middleton from the *Globe Democrat,*" I said, as I offered my
hand. "Good news for our nation's birthday yesterday!" He
looked thinner and more hollow-eyed, although there was still a
singleness of purpose in his face. As usual, his sandy hair was
uncombed, as though he had wrestled a rooster to see who
would announce the dawn. As was his custom, he wore even in
summer a bearskin overcoat.

"I been telling Old Abe we need more generals like Grant,"
Lane said, gesturing with his fist. "He don't pussyfoot around.
Got the goddamn Rebels on the run. Swarmed them thicker
than frogs in Egypt," he said emphatically.

"The Colored regiments also fought well at Cabin Creek," I responded, knowing he would not refuse credit for recruiting black

soldiers. "I congratulate you on giving them a chance to fight for their freedom."

"Heard they fought like devils . . . worked the Rebs like a stallion does a mare, I say . . . 'til his pizzle's limp." He gave a laugh, showing his teeth. "Any Secesh we capture need to stretch hemp, eh. That's the thing for traitors."

"May I attribute that sentiment to you, Senator?"

"You bet, though hanging's too good for them. Cut off their bollocks! Yep, you can say that too," he added in his characteristic harsh whisper. I would send the Senator's comments to Downing, who enjoyed Lane's ejaculations, especially if they contained a solecism or impropriety.

Stopping for a minute on the board sidewalk outside Ridenour and Baker's—a grocery which compared favorably with the finest I had seen in the East—I listened to the stonemasons finishing the footings of the bridge across the Kaw, a task made easier by the reduced summer flow of the river. The flag on the tall Liberty Pole at the end of Massachusetts Street hung lifeless in the still August morning. Nearby stood Henry Sonnet talking to the pastor of our church, Reverend Richard Cordley. "Saw you with the Senator," Henry said as I approached them. "Been watching work on the bridge."

"Should have the bridge finished by the time the Pacific Railroad gets the track laid to North Lawrence," Cordley exclaimed. "The railroad will be an economic blessing."

"Railroad may put me *out* of business," Henry said with a hearty laugh. "Well, what's Lane up to now?"

"Vengeance on Missourians, I guess," I replied. "I don't know if he cares whether they're loyal or not."

"Surely he means action only against secessionist partisans," Cordley said hopefully, before adding, "not loyalists."

"Not sure the Senator always sees the difference," I said, and Henry chuckled. "My editor loves stories about Lane, but now I need to speak with General Ewing about his plans to keep the bushwhackers out of Kansas. Could be a good story for the *Globe Democrat.*"

Many now thought the war was almost over. A giddy optimism swept over Lawrence: Union victories at Gettysburg and

Vicksburg and the recent appointment of General Thomas
Ewing, Jr., a thirty-three year old brigadier general to command
the District of the Border, a man of energy and promise, who established a chain of garrisons intended to stem the flow of
predatory bands, arrested and gaoled the families and friends of
suspected guerrillas in whatever buildings were available, and
declared martial law.

Then, shockingly, on August thirteenth, an unsound brick
detention building on Grand Avenue in Kansas City collapsed,
killing five women and crippling several more. Knowing how unfortunate events could spark retaliations, I set off for Kansas
City four days later and there learned the names of the victims,
among them Bill Anderson's sister and Coleman Younger's
cousin, both men leaders of the bushwhackers. I arranged to
leave Hannah and the children under the watchful eyes of Henry
and Leona, thinking I might be away from home for three or four
days while I learned of Ewing's plans for the Border.

Young Ewing had impressed the Kansas City papers like the
Western Journal of Commerce, and he spoke with a calm effi-
ciency and confidence. He explained that one day after the
building had collapsed, he had signed General Order No. Ten:
the forced removal of families of suspected guerrillas from four
counties in far western Missouri, banishing several thousand
persons from their homes. This action would be met with scorn
in Missouri but relief and joy in Kansas. The collapse of the detention building had received little notice in the Kansas City
papers; I seemed to be wrong to fear repercussions from the incident.

Having gathered the information I needed for Downing, I
called on General Ewing again in his headquarters, Pacific
House, the finest hotel in Kansas City, the evening of August
twentieth. Depopulating the Missouri counties already ravaged
by the Jayhawkers would remove the aid and support that allowed the bushwhackers to raid across the border, he said
forcefully. He was confident that the cycle of reprisal and vendetta was at last at an end. I thanked the General, bade him
good night, and sat in the hotel's elegant lobby to complete the
story which before leaving town I would telegraph to Downing.

The hotel was the one Thomas Pidgeon, the Colt Fire-Arms representative with the melodious voice, frequented in Kansas City, but that evening, as on several other occasions over the years when I inquired, no one knew or remembered the name. Even after sunset, the hotel was stifling, with no breeze stirring in the fetid street, the Missouri River below the town adding to the oppressiveness of the air. Once in the trap that would take me to Westport, with the wind in my face as we bounced down the rural roads, I experienced a welcome sense of wellbeing. My days of writing for Downing were surely coming to an end as the conflicts in Kansas and Missouri were rolled up, as Ewing expected would happen, and the Federal armies, at last, prevailed across the country. Perhaps with news traveling quickly by telegraphy, weekly papers like the *Globe Democrat* would not long survive the war.

Without the monthly salary from Downing, I needed to build up my legal practice, which I could certainly do since I was known and respected in town. Then, too, I still had the goal of writing a novel like Mr. Melville's *Moby Dick*. In the West, I had known heroes and rascals, observed natural and man-made disasters, and seen the best and worst of human nature. Perhaps in my experience, I could find an Ahab, Hamlet, or even a devilish Iago.

To escape the blazing sun on my ride back to Lawrence on the morrow, I would leave Westport well before dawn on Friday with my two horses, one carrying my full saddle bags. I was eager again to spend a night with my wife, and I would carry in my pocket peppermints as a treat for my children. Since both horses were well rested, I could make good time and arrive home by mid-morning.

CHAPTER FIFTEEN

By the time I came over the hill outside Eudora—the hamlet
five miles east of Lawrence—I knew something was wrong. Above
the horizon to the west, thick smoke hung in the still morning
air; not the smoke of a farmer's field being burned off or a single
house afire. All of Lawrence was on fire! Bushwhackers!
Quantrill! Terror gripped my heart as I kicked my horse into a
gallop, the pack horse following. Behind me, the sun was already far above the horizon, in front of me clouds of black and
silver spiraling upward and spreading like fog. As I raced down
the California Road, the scene ahead looked peaceful enough:
cornfields and a few grazing cattle. Was I too far away for gunfire
to be heard? I looked back and forth in front of me—only open
fields. No riders. I could not allow myself to think about my family.

I have heard it said that in times of personal peril, one's life
may pass before him like a visual narrative, but in my mind's
eye as I rode furiously, bent forward over my horse's neck, I saw
no scenes from my history, but rather faces in moments of time:
Hannah, who had described herself as a maiden never bold but
who defied convention in society and regularly surprised me
with her audacity in our most intimate moments; my dead father, who cared for me as *both* father and mother, educating me
at great cost and then accepting my choice of unorthodox career; my face as a youth, a lover of well-crafted words, who
preferred to stand behind the curtain and speak briefly to the
purpose, unseen; Russell Downing, who encouraged me to write
honestly, without rancor or partisan bias, always letting the
truth govern the story; Charles Robinson, who envisioned a Holy
City, a New Jerusalem on the Kansas plains but who would not
be allowed to build it; Jim Hickok, who was as handsome as a
Greek god and in his heroic feats lived like one, seeking

adventure, the more dangerous the more satisfying; John Brown, the devout Calvinist for whom the God-ordained cause, and *only* the cause, mattered; Henry Sonnet, a second father, who had made a man out of a callow and ineffectual greenhorn, teaching me the skills to survive on the frontier; and my babies, from whom I learned tenderness.

Of all these, one face I kept before me, Hannah's, her face as sharp and distinct as a daguerreotype with her look of pride and defiance when our eyes first met. I could not now allow my fear and anger to rule me, and I found hope in the sack of Lawrence in May of '56—the day of my arrival in town—when no one was injured or killed and only property was destroyed, the Free State Hotel and the two free-soil newspapers. Perhaps the correspondence would hold and again buildings alone would be affected, not the inhabitants. As I drew nearer to town, I saw no sign of raiders, no riders fleeing eastward toward Missouri.

The day was already hot; I was sweating and my horse tiring, the second horse, set free, had been left behind. Now I felt the acrid smoke in my nostrils as did my horse, who jerked his head in protest. As I left the road and cut across unfenced fields and pasture, I noticed the fresh tracks of a large company of riders who had crossed the fields ahead of me, riding toward the town—a company of frightening size. A barn to my left had been torched and was still in flames, and the nearby house seemed abandoned. I was close enough now to see the flames through the heavy smoke over what had been a beautiful town, now an inferno like Dante's. Since I heard no gunshots, I assumed the raiders had fled, perhaps south down the Fort Scott Road, swinging back toward Missouri. Nearing Fifteenth Street, the southern edge of town, I touched my Colt revolver in the holster on my thigh, still urging my lathered horse forward. The houses on the edge of town, widely scattered, had not been burned and several people now cautiously peered at me from places of safety.

The shortest route would take me over fields and straight down Rhode Island to my home on Eighth; two blocks away on Massachusetts every building seemed in flames. Pulling my kerchief over my nose as I entered a bank of smoke, I could see a body, two women tending to a wounded or dead husband or father. Of the three houses on Rhode Island, one was burned down but I could see as I jumped off my dead-weary horse that our house was standing, unharmed, smoke seeming to come from the stable. I was screaming Hannah's name as I ran to the back door.

"Ezra! It's Ezra!" I yelled as I pounded on the door. I could hear our dog, Caesar, barking frantically inside. "Open the door! It's Ezra!"

The door swung open and there was Hannah, her hair down and my shotgun in hand, laughing through tears. "You're safe," she said. "Thank God, you're safe. They came to kill you."

"Well, don't *you* shoot me then, Hannah," I said, holding her in my arms. "You and the babies? None of you hurt?"

"He had a list," she said, controlling her sobs. "Said he'd send you . . . to join John Brown in Hell. When he couldn't find you," she stopped, breathing hard, then continued, "said he'd burn the house down but something in the street distracted him. I would kill him if he came back. I had the shotgun from the closet."

"They're gone now," I reassured her. "Saw smoke when I rode up. Is the stable on fire?"

"When the devil left, I set a match to some rags in the wash tub. Tried to fool them into thinking . . . we were already on fire," she replied, still breathing heavily.

"You saved our house," I said, calmer now, although my heart still pounded in my chest.

"Oh, Ezra," she said pulling back from me. "I fear for Henry and Leona. Most of the houses on New Hampshire are burned, I think." Hands to her face, she shook her head. "Henry must have been on a list!" I ran to the bedroom to reassure little Samantha, who was crying. Henley was still asleep. I gave Samantha a kiss and hurried out. Behind me, I could hear Hannah locking the door.

My horse stood at the water trough outside the stable, exhausted, waiting to be unsaddled; nearby Hannah's washtub of smoldering rags added to the miasma of smoke and stink, but I was already running north. Between our house and the Sonnets stood open ground, planted in vegetables, treeless except for the small maple by Sonnet's barn, so I could see that, although his barn seemed sound, the house was smoking, charred timbers. Several of Sonnet's mules in the barn brayed for food and water and as I ran closer, I saw the horrible sight I had feared: Leona standing by the barn door, her nightdress soaked in blood.

"Are you hurt?" I panted as I ran up to her.

"Shot him like a dog, Ezra," she said, tears running down her face, but still able to command a strong voice. "Three of them. Laughed when they shot him. Like fiends from Hell, they were."

I put my arm around her and walked with her to the barn. Inside lay Henry on his back. A trail of black blood showed where his wife had dragged him across the dirt yard. She had placed a blanket over him, covering his face, but his bare feet protruded. "Oh, Ezra, forgive me. I didn't ask about Hannah and the children!"

"All safe . . . and the house," I replied, finding a horse blanket to put around her shoulders—for decency's sake, not warmth, since the day was already hot. "I'm taking you there now, if you can walk across the fields on bare feet." She nodded, happy to have someone tell her what to do. "Where's Black Bob and Isaac?"

"Will Henry be all right laying there?" she asked, walking away with me, turning to look back.

"Yes, yes. I'll hitch up the mules and bring him to our house. Lucky the Rebels left the mules. Bet they took all the good horses in town." I didn't tell her I had plans for the mules and the wagon: someone would have to collect the fly-covered bodies, however many there were—perhaps dozens—before they began to putrefy in the sun.

Seeing my murdered friend lying in the dust had clarified my thoughts, and my anger had given me strength. My mind was working like an engine—a gin which moved or lifted or separated with the turn of a dial or crank. I could see what needed to be done and in what order.

"Bob's in Leavenworth. Due back today," Leona said, remembering my question. "Isaac has fled to safety, I hope. Expect they shot Negroes on sight."

"Let's hope they didn't destroy the ferry," I replied, and Leona mumbled a response. "Bob will need it to get the wagon across the river." Walking slowly with her, I could see that about half the houses on New Hampshire had been torched; on Rhode Island, several houses were burned, and now I realized that Zeke Skinner, my neighbor, was lying dead and bloody outside what had been his front door, part of his head gone. I hoped Leona hadn't seen him.

Hannah was outside looking for us, still carrying the shotgun, having put my horse in the stable. I remembered what Henry had often said: *Always take care of your horse before yourself, Ezra.* Hannah came to us and helped Leona into the house, and I went to give the children the peppermints I had bought in Kansas City, still wrapped in paper in my pocket. Samantha, who had celebrated her fourth birthday before I left for Kansas City and my interview with Ewing, had heard the gunfire and noise and was still frightened. Telling Hannah, I would bring Henry's body to our house, I left again as she returned to Leona.

When I approached Sonnet's barn, stopping near the maple tree beneath which Henry planned to sit in an old age he would never have, I heard a noise and, thinking perhaps a raider, injured and left behind, was trying to steal the mules, I drew my Colt revolver and shouted, "Come out of there. I've got a pistol and it's cocked."

A young voice came from inside. "It's Isaac, Mr. Ezra. I'm here with Mr. Sonnet."

"Isaac?" I asked as the familiar face emerged from the shadows. "Are you fit and sound?" Fear was in the boy's eyes as he approached, and I holstered my gun. "You're safe now. Can you help me today?" The boy swallowed and nodded, unsure what I expected of him. "Black Bob should be back from Leavenworth soon—if he can get across the river." Isaac nodded again.

"I found Mr. Henry inside the barn," he explained—now grown much taller, five years since Hannah and Leona began to school him.

"Old wagon still behind the barn, Isaac?" He mumbled a response and nodded again. "If you bring it around, I'll hitch up the mules." As I went for them, I thought Isaac was living up to his name, which was "Worthy." It must have taken great courage for a young black to stay near rather than run to the river to hide. We lifted Henry into the wagon, the dried blood on his nightshirt black and ugly, a feed sack under his head where Isaac had placed it in a tender gesture.

As we rode up Rhode Island, we saw women carrying buckets of water to throw on houses that still burned. I could see no men at all. Where were they? As Isaac and I placed the body on our dinner table, I said to Leona: "If we can find a coffin, Henry can be buried tomorrow." I noticed that her hair was now pinned up and she wore one of Hannah's dresses, although it didn't seem to fit well. She smiled at me. "We'll see what's happened downtown." Hannah gave Isaac and me cups of water. I hadn't realized how thirsty I was. "Sweetheart, can you tend to my horse?"

"Already unsaddled and fed him," she replied, smiling. "You take care now."

When Isaac and I reached Ninth, the south border of the commercial district, I saw a scene of horror which I could not have imagined in my most feverish nightmare. To my left on New Hampshire had been the camp where recruits, boys younger than Isaac, were learning to drill in uniform with mock weapons; now weeping women, like gleaners in a field at harvest, moved among ripped-down tents and twisted limbs to see if any of them were alive in this shambles.

On Massachusetts every building was afire. The stench of death was in the air—the smell of blood and burned flesh. Bodies filled the streets and sidewalks like a battlefield, and a few women looked to assist any living among the dead, fallen where they were shot. Fires burned in cellars like the furnaces of Hades. My mules feared the fires, but I urged them forward until I noticed old Petersen, the first living man I had seen in town.

"Ezra! Thank God!" he called out. "Ain't no men left. Women are trying to put out the fires."

Handing the reins to Isaac, I jumped down. "Any of them alive?" I asked. Some were so horribly burned it was impossible to know if they were black or white, all equal in death. Scattered among the bodies were items from looted stores: boxes, shirts and hats, empty whiskey jugs, and food cans. Some walls of blackened brick were still standing. "Where are the injured taken?"

"Methodist Church," Petersen answered, moving to turn over a body. "Can't recognize ones I know, so badly burned. Their skin just slips off the body. Threw up first time that happened."

"Let's start getting bodies up to the church," I said, and Petersen, an old man with surprising strength, helped me lift four bodies into the wagon. The day was hot, and the stench of the blood was suffocating. Isaac and I led the mules, which were becoming harder to handle, toward the Methodist Church, its roof and steeple undamaged, a street away.

Edna Fuller, a friend of Hannah's, had taken charge in the church. "Thank God, you're alive, Ezra," she said, taking my hand in hers. "There are no coffins, no cabinetmakers. Told the women to bring in whatever they could to make shrouds. Did I do the right thing, do you think?" She chattered nervously, not stopping for a response. "Reverend Paddock's here helping with the wounded. There's a doctor too—Virgil Gafney. New in town."

"Yes, you did well," I responded to her question, looking around the church sanctuary, which had been cleared of furniture. A few wrapped bodies were lined up against one wall, a name or number pinned to each one. A German stonemason who had worked on the bridge helped to wrap the bodies, and I saw Paddock bandaging the injured in one corner. Twenty or so wounded were lying on the floor, and it was so hot inside the room I found it difficult to breathe.

Coming outside, I saw Isaac giving water to the mules. "See if you can pick up more bodies on Massachusetts while I try to find Judge Carpenter." We needed someone to take command and Louis Carpenter, although still young, was a respected citizen and jurist who lived not far from the Sonnets. Had I the speed of wing-footed Mercury and the strength of mighty Hercules, I could not have attended to all that needed doing that day. Again, I ran through the streets until I reached the Carpenters' house on New Hampshire; it had not burned. Mary Carpenter stood with her sister, Abigail; the Judge lay in blood at their feet.

"Is the Judge alive?" I asked running up. Mary was kneeling by the body, so Abigail answered me.

"They shot him," Abigail spoke through her tears. "Just shot him. Had four or five pistols apiece stuck in their waistbands. Mary tried to shield him when he fell. They pulled her arm away and shot him in the head."

"Do you want us to take him to the Methodist Church with the others?" I asked, raising Mary to her feet. Abigail thrust a crude map of the town at me. On it were these words: *who we want* and *judge.*

"Dropped the map when they killed him," Mary said, holding her handkerchief to her face. "We'll bury him where he fell."

"Then let me carry him inside for you to lay out," I said, and taking the Judge under his arms and Abigail his feet, we carried him inside. Such a waste, this talented young man, my good friend. "I must go now. I'm so sorry." The women thanked me, gracious in tragedy, and Abigail kissed my blood-stained hands. Every victim increased my rage and my grief but I could not indulge myself in passion when so many felt even greater loss than did I, parted from members of their families forever.

Down New Hampshire I saw Black Bob O'Hare's mule-drawn freight wagon coming from the ferry; I waved to him and thanked the Lord for his return. Bob had jumped down from the wagon near the ruins of the Sonnets' house when I ran up to him.

"Henry's dead. Leona's at my house," I said, out of breath. "Isaac's safe and he's in Henry's wagon picking up bodies."

"How many were killed, Ezra?" Black Bob demanded.

"Too many to count," I answered. "Glad to see *you* though."

"Got across on the ferry." He wiped his forehead with his bandana. Sweat poured from his heavy black beard and thick hair. "There are a few troopers on the far side of the river who kept the Secesh away from the ferry. On guard duty at the Delaware Indian Reserve, likely." He paused and looked at me. "Let me put this freight in Henry's barn."

"Don't know how many are dead, but I fear we're far short of the coffins we need. Maybe have to put bodies in a common grave." We talked as we unloaded wooden boxes from his wagon. The wood of some of these might be used for coffins. Then Bob got his reluctant mules moving.

On Massachusetts, I noted that more men had come out of hiding. "I wonder if they killed Lane or Mayor Collamore," Black Bob mused, "or Governor Robinson. There! Let's pick up these bodies too," he said, stopping the mules as we drove up to the blackened skeleton of the four-story Eldridge House, pieces of twisted wrought iron railing, like black tree limbs from the Nether World of Hades, poking up from the ashes. In the cellar, fires still burned, emitting sounds as walls collapsed or metal cooled. Two bodies, badly charred, lay by what had been the front door. We lifted them into the wagon.

Several soldiers in Union-blue uniforms arrived, perhaps the ones from across the river. Then Hannah and another woman came with jugs of water and a basket of cold cornbread and slices of fresh melon. The blazing sun told us it was past noon as the workers wolfed down the meager dinner. When Bob and I came around the still-burning ruins of the hotel and turned south to the white-washed Methodist Church on Vermont with our cargo, we saw the churchyard overflowing with the dead and wounded, bodies, many covered by horseflies drawn by the smell of blood, waiting to be interred on the morrow.

Down Vermont came the prosperous cattle agent Dan Cornish driving a wagon filled with food and blankets. Because he lived near the Wakarusa River south of town, I feared the retreating raiders might have attacked or burned his buildings.

"Any harm done to you, Dan?" I shouted as he jumped down from his wagon and wiped his face with his kerchief.

"Went right down the Fort Scott Road, crossed Blanton's Bridge, and burned Brooklyn to the ground . . . then headed east toward Paola and the Missouri line." Several women and boys were unloading his wagon as he spoke: bread, several hams, and melons. "A bit of shooting as they rode nearby. Lots of smoke but I didn't set eyes on them, thank the Lord."

Nor did I," I replied. I could tell Cornish was shocked by the dead and wounded. "It was Quantrill. Many are dead—shot or burned." He ran to the church and hurried inside.

Then I saw the white head of Richard Cordley, pastor of the Congregational Church, in whose magnificent library I had spent many evenings discussing books. "Richard," I said. "Thank God you're safe. And your family?"

"All safe. And Hannah and your children?"

"Yes, safe, but Henry Sonnet was killed," I said quietly as Cordley embraced me. Pleased though I was that the Cordleys were alive, rage still burned inside me like caustic soda.

"God rest his soul," the pastor said. "A good man. Saw you with Cornish. Glad the Lord delivered him too."

"How did you escape?" I asked and he seemed to smile, a sad expression of weariness more than merriment, and ran his hand up into his thin hair.

"The Lord preserved us—wife, child, and friend—as we ran through the street and reached the river. I thought we were trapped but a member of our congregation saw us from the north bank of the Kaw, rowed over at great risk to himself, and carried us to safety."

"I'll tell Hannah of your deliverance," I said, "when I next see her." I thought about a question that had bothered me all day: whom does God decide to deliver? So much seems to be a matter of chance, mere accident. Was I spared as part of God's plan or simply because I didn't come home a day earlier? I wondered whether I was losing my faith.

"Have you seen Mayor Collamore? The Senator?" Cordley asked.

"Haven't been to West Lawrence—anywhere past the ravine," I replied. The ravine was a steep, bosky gorge a block west of Vermont and the Methodist Church; a single wooden bridge carried traffic to West Lawrence, where a few large and elegant houses stood, bounded by large cornfields which ran to the foot of Mount Oread, fields in which I waited when the Border Ruffians threatened the town in'56.

"Ezra, could you take your wagon down to the Governor's to see if they could provide succor for the wounded here?" He

swept his hand toward the wounded lying in the sun on stretch-
ers or sitting against the church, attended by women in dirty
clothing. "His house wasn't burned. Some houses near the ferry
and the Liberty Pole survived; I don't know how!"

"A few Federal troops were across the Kaw," I said. "Sharp-
shooters in trees would have killed any bushwhackers who tried
to burn the houses. Must have been trying to protect the ferry, I
guess."

"I'm certain Robinson could supply blankets or bandages or
food—anything." Cordley's eyes searched my face for confirma-
tion.

"He will be charitable," I said, hurrying to see if Black Bob
had unloaded the wagon. I knew Robinson was bitter after the
campaign which had driven him from office and destroyed his
reputation, and Sara, his wife, was known to be resentful. Bob
was drinking a cup of water, bloody as a surgeon after taking off
a limb, but he jumped into the wagon and turned the mules
around. Henry always said Bob knew the mind of the mule better than anyone on the prairie.

Away from the smoke and burning timbers of the buildings,
we passed the Armory—its doors still intact—and found that
only one of the dozen or so houses at the foot of Massachusetts
Street was touched by fire. These were mansions as fine as
those in West Lawrence, stone or brick, with spacious lawns. I
ran to the Governor's door and dropped the brass knocker,
sending a plangent sound echoing through the house. The door
swung open and Robinson peered at me uncertainly.

"Ezra Middleton," he said with a grim face. "A tragic day. Glad
you survived."

"Yes, many have died today, Governor," I responded, taking
the hand he offered me. Because we had a cordial relationship, I
believed he would hear my desperate plea. "Scores of wounded
or dying at the Methodist Church, sir. We need blankets, coffins,
food . . . water."

"I saw it all—from Mount Oread. Had taken my quotidian
drive to my old barn. . . But let me have Sara get food and drink
for you. I have no coffins, of course."

"Some canvas perhaps or packing crates." But Robinson had scurried from the room to seek his wife. In a few moments, he returned.

"Have your driver take his wagon to the back."

When I returned to thank Robinson, after speaking to Black Bob, the Governor handed me two apples. "I began to tell you of my drive up Mount Oread in the cool of the morning. I like to watch the sun come up." I could see grief in his face as he spoke. "I saw it all, Ezra, from the dust cloud as the riders left the California Road—riding in formation four abreast like a cavalry unit, a few heading the column in Union jackets, stolen, I assume." He looked me in the eye. "But no flag—no squadron flag. So, I knew it was Quantrill."

"And nothing you could do to stop it."

"They paused at South Park," he said. "Must have been four hundred. Formed into three groups. Went down the main streets, the middle one straight to the Eldridge House, shooting and yelling. Massachusetts was a shooting gallery—merchants shot down as they came out into the street. Then the shops were set ablaze—terrible beyond words!" He paused, overcome by grief and the memory of the slaughter, observed from on high like a god on Olympus.

"It must be horrible for you, Governor. This is *your* town, but you couldn't save it today."

"Just so, Ezra." I was certain there were tears in his pale eyes. "Come back in a few days. You must tell the country in your paper. The horrors we have seen."

"Yes, I shall. Thank you for . . .." He cut me off.

"On your way now, "he said, ushering me out. Black Bob was pulling the wagon up in front and I jumped in, not forgetting to hand him one of the apples.

"Watched his town being destroyed from atop Mount Oread, Bob," I said, biting into my apple. The wagon was piled with all manner of things. The Robinsons had been generous.

At the church, I turned the supplies over to Paddock. It was late in the afternoon—still hot, smelly, and noisy. Then I saw my friend Edmund Whitman, land agent, farmer, and ardent abolitionist. It was at his farm a few miles from Lawrence that on a cold and snowy day I had met with John Brown and some of his followers in November of '57.

"Ezra," he shouted and came over. "Dirty and bloody, aren't you?"

"Not *my* blood, Ed," I said. "Have you come to help? We can use it!"

"Brought food and clothing. You may remember my son," he added, pausing. "Wanted to pursue Quantrill with Lane's posse . . . so, I brought him here with me."

"Lane's alive?" I asked incredulously, realizing as I asked the question that if anyone could survive the attack it would be Lane.

"Way I heard it, Lane's mansion was looted and burned but Lane escaped in his nightshirt and hid in his cornfield. After all the raiders left, he came sneaking out and organized a posse to chase them down."

"But are there any good horses left in town?" I asked. "I hear Quantrill went out of here with a huge remuda—all fresh horses."

"That's the point, isn't it?" Whitman laughed. "The posse's mounted on old mules, plow horses. And the riders are Lane's toadies, shop keepers, and boys, carrying old muskets and farm tools. I don't want Lane getting my son killed . . . or my good horses either. But the posse won't catch the bushwhackers on their fresh mounts."

Whitman waved his arm as if to scatter the posse himself. "Besides, that's the job of the cavalry, isn't it? Must be on Quantrill's heels now, trying to cut him off before he can get back into Missouri."

"I'm thinking of Lane's posse," I said, beginning to snicker and, struggling with exhaustion, broke out in laughter I could not stifle. Whitman frowned at me and my behavior. I imagined Senator Lane like the comic figure Don Quixote on his bony nag, tilting at windmills he thought giants—bouncing across the prairie on a spavin horse, shouting and waving a rusty musket, and on his head in place of Quixote's helmet a chamber pot. People glared at me: those giving water to the injured, fanning the tired in the heat of the late afternoon, or easing the pain of burns or gunshot wounds. I wanted to apologize—but I could not stop laughing.

CHAPTER SIXTEEN

Black Friday, everyone in Lawrence called the twenty-first of August. On the street, they would greet one another: *How'd you fare on Black Friday?* And they would date events as *two days before Black Friday* or *three days since Black Friday*, setting a calendar of memories which they would henceforth live by.

When I awoke on Saturday, the weight of tasks to be performed pressed on my chest like a millstone: burial of the dead before contagion spread among the living, food for man and beast, shelter for the homeless, and care for the injured. I sat at breakfast with Hannah and Leona, eating stale biscuits and drinking fresh milk from our cow, gloom as oppressive in the room as the smell of the burned wood that seeped through the cracks and under the doors.

"I'm not going to sell Henry's freight line," Leona said quietly, as though doing so had been a subject of discussion. "Way I see it, carrying freight will have a favored place when the whole town is rebuilding. I know Henry's partners in Kansas City and Leavenworth, and we already have mules and wagons at Westport." She smiled uncertainly at us, but her jawline looked strong, determined. "Now is the time to add *wholesale,* especially with the Union Pacific coming next year. That's what Henry would do." Nothing except seeing the severed heart of Quantrill on my knife's point could have cheered me more. Giving Leona and Hannah each a hug, I left to meet Black Bob and form a burial detail. At the church, Eli Foster and Isaac Worthy joined us.

Reverend Cordley and I tried to record the events of the massacre and count the losses. Although a number of persons were still missing, the number of dead we believed to be more than one hundred and fifty. Three more were added to the total when Mayor George Collamore and two would-be rescuers were found drowned or perhaps suffocated in Collamore's well in West Lawrence. Cordley's total included seventeen Union recruits who had been slaughtered as they struggled to leave their tents, although most if not all the black recruits on Massachusetts had managed to escape their camp and hide in the willow groves along the river. The pastor also thought about one hundred homes had been destroyed. Wagons were now carrying the dead, some in makeshift coffins, other bodies in shrouds, up Mount Oread to the cemetery.

A relief convoy from Leavenworth arrived by mid-day with food, clothing—and a few coffins—and aid came too from local farmers. In the cellars of some buildings, embers still glowed and crackled. Fortunately, two hotels had not been torched and the vault of one of the three banks could not be opened by the raiders, but Lawrence had been stripped of its wealth as its citizens were being put to slaughter.

Grief over Henry's death fathered my anger, which was increased by my inability to strike back at the Secesh bushwhackers. On Saturday afternoon I learned that one—but only one—of the Rebels had lost his life, a drunken lout named Larkin Skaggs, whose naked corpse had been dragged down Massachusetts by a black man. I had no expectation that Lane could inflict vengeance on the murderers or recover any of the stolen property, but as we worked at our grisly task during the hot afternoon, more and more gravediggers talked of the future and how Lawrence would rebuild. Word also came that two victims—John Thornton and Harlow Baker, part owner of R and B's—once near death, had improved and would live.

Sunday dawned with continued heat as I hitched the mules to the buggy which would carry Hannah and me to church, Leona having offered to mind the children. I wore a clean shirt and collar for the first time since Friday and for the first time since the raid I heard birds singing. The service was unusually short and solemn with a reading from Scripture, Psalms 79: *O God, the heathen have come into thine inheritance. They have laid Jerusalem in ruins. They have given the bodies of thy servants unto the birds of the air and the flesh of thy saints unto the beasts of the earth. Their blood they have poured out like water all around Jerusalem, and there was no one to bury them.*

Because they had nothing else, many of the worshippers still wore the clothing they had put on Friday morning, now stained with blood as black as the overalls of a locomotive fireman. I tried to pray but could not, anger so fierce in my blood. What would Charles Robinson think of Cordley's verse from the Psalms? Did the next verse suggest how Jerusalem could be rebuilt or how its inhabitants could recover? Neither Hannah nor I said a word as we rode through the ruined town. Taking off and folding my clean shirt and donning a stained one, I returned to the makeshift mortuary at the Methodist church. Eli was already there, his curly blond hair a reminder of happier times together.

In the afternoon I noticed the arrival of writers and illustrators from the newspapers, easy to identify by their clean clothes and faces, and I knew they would describe the victims in the most exaggerated and lurid language for their readers in the East. When one writer asked me how to describe the stench of the putrefying flesh, I cursed him, shouting a phrase from the law: *"Res ipsa loquitur,"* that is, *the matter speaks for itself.* "Use your fucking nose!" Sweating in his black frock coat under the white-hot sun, cousin to the inky turkey buzzards floating above the town, he looked at me in puzzlement.

My account for Downing would not limn the bodies or charred timbers but would record the bravery of the citizens of Lawrence. I heard of women who saved husbands from certain death at the bushwhackers' hands by dressing them in long dresses and bonnets and slowly walking away from burning houses or, still under threat from the marauders, returning repeatedly to throw water on fires. Elizabeth Fisher hid her husband Hugh in the space between the kitchen floor and cellar but needing to move him when the house was set ablaze, wrapped him in a carpet which she dragged outside and, under the gaze of the Rebels, calmly sat on the singed carpet until they rode away. Another husband was carried to safety, hidden in a feather bed. At almost every burning house a woman poured water on a fire or helped a wounded or dying husband.

Late in the day, however, a north wind blew, clearing the air of both odor and ash, but our terrible task, consuming all our energy, continued into the night as we carried bodies by lantern light like a ghostly company of monks burying plague-stricken brothers. Since individual graves could not be dug fast enough, a long trench was started that could accommodate numerous bodies—by my count, we there buried forty-seven. Moving with haste and exhaustion before the impending storm, I had the mules fed and stabled as the hurricane hit with the fury of the storm in *King Lear*—lightning that crackled across the black sky, thunder that rumbled and roared, cold rain as cruel as bullets—and I understood for the first time the Bard's portrait of the poor naked wretches who had to abide the fury of the pitiless storm. Earlier, Leona had killed one of our chickens and baked it, and we ate it at midnight—gratefully in the warm and dry kitchen.

Monday brought a pleasant change, a sky cloudless and bright, and I decided to forego the brief interments and truncated memorials to write the story for Downing, the weekly issue of the paper perhaps already waiting at the press. With details in mind, I wrote quickly, feeling the pain of grief but holding to my intent to tell the story accurately. This had been a brutal act of war by Confederate outlaws, not just a vengeful action by Missourians against Kansans, as Jim Lane was charging after his futile chase, as he offered the raid as a pretext for an invasion of Missouri. Dan Cornish agreed with me that the opportunistic Lane must not be allowed to use the tragedy for his own dark ambitions.

I had just finished my writing when the first knock at the door made me realize that attorneys are as much needed after a disaster as undertakers or haulers of freight. I would have no trouble ginning up my legal business when insurance claims, property disputes, and new wills all called for action. When my clients left and I made a fair copy of my story, I blotted it and gave it to the new driver who had been hired to carry mail and freight to and from Leavenworth, Larby Jones; he would have the story telegraphed to Downing.

On Tuesday, Jones returned, carrying copies of the *Leaven-worth Daily Conservative*, with the most current information on the prairie. And the news was important: General Thomas Ewing, Jr.—now widely blamed because his defensive plan for Kansas had failed—had taken a bold step to deflect criticism, a new General Order.

Whereas Order No. Ten removed the families of known or suspected bushwhackers from Missouri counties along the Border, Order No. Eleven decreed that *all* persons in those counties were to be expelled, although a few persons who could prove themselves loyal might be allowed to remain in towns. Fields were to be burned, shelters of any kind torn down, and livestock confiscated. Although many loyal Missourians protested, the Kansas followers of Jim Lane, Doc Jennison, and George Hoyt, leader of the Red Legs—Jayhawkers known for their scarlet gaiters—cheered and demanded more. I anticipated receipt of the *Globe Democrat* to see Downing's editorial about this new General Order and—I must confess it—how much of my wooly story on the Lawrence Massacre had survived Downing's merciless shears.

Because Governor Robinson had suggested a return visit, that evening I walked through town to the bank of the Kansas or Kaw River and the mansions near the Liberty Pole, where now flew a new American flag. Robinson was forthcoming in presenting his views. Yes, Ewing's political hopes, so bright a week before, had been blackened like the skeletal buildings of the town, blackened beyond recovery. "I speak as an expert on tarnished reputation, Ezra," he said bitterly. His views on the late mayor, George Collamore, did not surprise me. "That little man was a big fool. Imagine having all those new rifles for the town watch locked in an armory that could not be opened," he laughed, "even by Quantrill and his raiders!" Then more quietly he added: "The stupid little man."

"Does seem to have outwitted himself, sir," I observed with a smile. Each of us had been poured a glass of whiskey and I sipped mine. Robinson was as usual well dressed, his beard neatly trimmed. Since I had been discussing legal matters with several clients, I was dressed in clean and pressed clothing.

"What figures are you using in the reports to your paper?" Cocking his head slightly, he fixed his gaze on me.

"I say about two hundred men and boys killed," I replied. "That includes twenty or so missing who may never be found. Germans who were working on the bridge—no one knows how many. Burned up, most likely." Robinson continued to watch me. "No women harmed, of course."

"Of course. Gentlemanly murderers indeed. Still, I'm glad no women were troubled."

"And so, Ewing's political ambitions have been nipped . . . plowed up . . . plowed under for good."

"Will you write that Ewing is to blame then? There was a false alarm as early as July 31 and three more on successive nights in August. Why were no watches set out after all the rumors? And why no soldiers stationed in the second largest town in Kansas?"

"So, you lay all the blame on Ewing then?"

"On Ewing?" Robinson roared. "On Ewing?" he repeated, slapping his bald head. "By God, no! Not General Ewing or General Schofield or the Mayor—or the good Lord Jesus. I lay the blame where it belongs—on that villain Lane!"

Fearing he would suffer apoplexy, I held my breath and waited, looking away from the Governor's purple face. He was breathing heavily, eyes bulging like eggs, more agitated than I had ever seen him.

Assuring him I thought jayhawking had contributed to the vendettas that inflamed the frontier, I was nevertheless embarrassed by my equivocation and quickly added that doubtless, Lane bore some blame. "Our people are easily led by a rabblerouser," I conceded, but Robinson's anger seemed already to have burned itself out.

"I forgot myself, Ezra," he said. "Forgive me."

As I walked back through the town, I thought about the question in *King Lear: Is there any cause in nature that makes these hard hearts?* Of course, the play provides no answer about where the evil in man originates. In matters of politics and government, however, pernicious institutions can and do have deadly consequences. I could see how the evils of slavery had corrupted the body politic and the instruments of government, and I knew that civil slaughter would continue until slavery was extirpated. Madman or prophet, John Brown had been right. As I passed the spot where the recruits had been shot, a white tent now stood with the word "Enlistment" affixed to it.

When I reached home, Leona was reading to Samantha and, with Henley already in bed, Hannah sewed by a brass kerosene lamp, the windows open despite the lingering odor of charred wood. Dogs were again barking in the streets and pigs, I had no doubt, were again rooting for garbage on the side streets.

When Samantha had been put to bed, I sat with the women at the kitchen table. "The town is coming back to life, but much is unchanged," I said. "Robinson will bear his scars, still believing Kansas would have been stronger—indeed, Lawrence would not have suffered . . ." I stopped because the name of Henry Sonnet was about to come to my lips and my affections overwhelmed me. "If Lane had not destroyed the governor," I added lamely. "But whether I write for a paper or practice the law, I must do what I can so that justice and respect for law prevail here." Both women watched me. "But before that can happen, the enemies of the Union must be defeated once and for all. Free the slaves, yes, but first preserve the Union, just as Lincoln says. I've struggled with this decision." The women still watched, waiting for my next words. "Forgive me, Hannah, for not seeking your assent but I cannot allow others to make sacrifices while I sit at home. Tomorrow I'm going to enlist in the state militia.

CHAPTER SEVENTEEN

Autumn came to the prairie, as it often does, with warm
breezes from the west and burnished sunlight glowing like polished brass. Yet in the season of dying vegetation, the people of
Lawrence watched the seeds of hope sprout into robust new
growth. Within a week, black men shoveled ashes from the cellars of stores along Massachusetts, and R and B's was already
selling merchandise from a tent behind the foundations of the
old store, most items no doubt bought on credit. Four prominent men had pledged $100,000 each to rebuild the Eldridge
House Hotel, and soon on almost every lot in the business district a new building was rising, often one of stone or brick
replacing one constructed of wood. At the center of the vortex of
activity was Leona Sonnet, whose freight wagons hauled materials from the brickyard and the new sawmill on the Kansas River
to the big barn on New Hampshire that had become "Henry Sonnet Freight and Wholesale."

Editor John Speer's new paper, *The Kansas Tribune*—a successor to his *Lawrence Republican*, burned down by the
marauders—chronicled the rebuilding of Lawrence: two new
banks, several livery stables, a dozen stores where groceries and
provisions were sold, two jewelers, eight saloons, two daguerreotype studios, a foundry and machine shop, four flour mills, a
brewery, and—across the river—a score of new homes in North
Lawrence. Now the new wooden bridge carried traffic over the
river and Lawrence awaited the arrival of the Pacific Railroad
and the telegraph line. Over the bridge would ride factors and
agents who could bring the town necessary skills and new enterprises.

Eclipsing the hope and optimism of recovery, however, like a
sinister cloud sliding across the sun, was a ghost called
Quantrill, for half the people of Lawrence believed that the

Confederate raider would return to create more heartbreak and horror. This fear persisted despite the fortification of the town: a stockade on Mount Oread called Camp Lookout, constructed of heavy logs where fifty men at a time were on guard day and night. In town, a network of trenches and breastworks recalled the days of John Brown in '56, and two blockhouses had now been built in the heart of town. Lawrence was a fortress and as a member of the Kansas militia, I was part of the force that guarded the town, each month spending several days and nights atop Mount Oread, in addition to what seemed like endless drills.

Although the state could not provide uniforms for the new enlistees, I felt like an infantryman as I became accustomed to the clink of brass, the smell of black powder, and the weight of my cartridge box and haversack. In my company were young boys I knew from the town: Jeremiah Whitman, son of my friend Ed, tall like his father, and Punky Paddock, son of the Methodist minister George Paddock—his name a shortening of "Pumpkin," for he possessed a large perfectly round head, his brown hair cropped close.

Because I was a dozen years older than many of the company, I became known as "Uncle Ezra." This jaunty name pleased me because I still carried within me a weight heavier than my equipment: grief and guilt from Black Friday. During the winter I followed news of the war in the East and South. The Confederacy was slowly being strangled. The Union navy controlled the sea and the Mississippi and on land, the Federal Army of the Cumberland had won major victories in Tennessee. By the close of 1863, the massive industrial output of the North and its much larger population made the outcome for the Confederacy seem bleak. It was only a matter of time we told ourselves.

Since the Border was secure, the winter of 1864 in Kansas was quiet, in large measure because the main bushwhacker companies—Quantrill's, Anderson's, and Todd's—were again wintering in Texas. But as the weather warmed in the spring, hundreds of these hardened Confederate irregulars were reported to be moving through the Indian Territory and Arkansas to gather in the deep and impenetrable woods east of Kansas City. In May, violence ripped through western Missouri as Union patrols were ambushed and unarmed Federal soldiers murdered, railroad carriages and stagecoaches robbed, steamboats on the Missouri River peppered by gunfire, and buildings burned in the night. For the state of Missouri, it was the bloodiest period of the war.

From the other side of the Border, I followed the destruction and terror in Missouri through the *Globe Democrat* and other regional newspapers. With so many calamitous events in his own state, Russell Downing had little need of my accounts and so I drilled and waited, spending what time was my own on legal efforts related to the rebuilding of Lawrence and on my family, which now included Leona.

It was not, however, a report of Quantrill or some other Rebel band which flashed across the prairie like a bolt of summer lightning but the news that a large Confederate army, its band playing and flags flying, had crossed the Arkansas River on September sixth, apparently heading for St. Louis, a metropolis which had heretofore been out of the path of invading armies.

Within a week the identity of these Secessionist interlopers was known across Missouri and Kansas: it was the Army of Missouri, commanded by Confederate Major General Sterling Price, consisting of three cavalry divisions and artillery, and estimated at ten to fifteen thousand men. General Price, "Pap" to his troops, was a former legislator, congressman, and governor of Missouri, once a tall, dashing, and dignified leader, but at fifty-five and now weighing almost three hundred pounds, forced to abandon his horse to ride in a mule-drawn carriage. He had commanded troops at Wilson's Creek and Pea Ridge, battles in which my friend Jim Hickok had also fought, as a sharp-shooter—on the Union side, of course. In the *Globe Democrat* Russell Downing speculated that Price had entered Missouri both to recruit soldiers from the bushwhacker companies and to plunder the rich military depot in St. Louis. If he could act swiftly and decisively to take St. Louis before the Federals brought up sufficient troops to oppose him, Price might prolong the war by months or even cross the Mississippi River to invade

Illinois. Downing thought the invasion a brilliant but risky venture, a desperate gamble. Sitting at home, I cursed my luck
because the Kansas militia would not be called up to fight in
eastern Missouri and I would lose perhaps my only chance to
seek vengeance for the massacre at Lawrence.

Moving northward, the Southern invaders caught a small Union force—as I learned from the Kansas City papers—at Pilot
Knob, where stood Fort Davidson, under the authority of
Thomas Ewing, Jr., an officer I remembered well as commander
of the Border in Kansas, blamed by many for failing to keep
Quantrill from reaching Lawrence. After two days of fierce
fighting, Ewing's triumphant garrison crept away during the
night. The Rebels then lost more valuable time in pursuit of the
retreating Ewing, leaving Price without the resources to attack
St. Louis, only forty miles away. For several days a panic had
swept over that city but quickly dissipated when it became obvious that the Rebel general had changed his plan. The accounts
suggested that Price, who had already blundered badly in his
campaign, was now forced to abandon his original objective and
march westward toward Jefferson City, the state capital.

In the meantime, Union Major General William S. Rosecrans,
commanding the Federal Department of Missouri, called up the
state militia and assembled his army. The newspapers speculated that Price was short of both supplies and men, the
bushwhackers he had hoped to recruit failing to materialize in
sufficient numbers. On October eighth, Price retreated from Jefferson City to continue to move toward Kansas City on the
state's western border. Now I eagerly combed any newspaper I
could find and talked to all the militia officers I knew to determine whether there might be a chance that Price's army would
get close enough to the Border for the Kansas militia to be called
out.

And calling out the Kansas militia was exactly what Major
General Samuel Ryan Curtis had demanded repeatedly late in
September, for General Curtis, commander of the Federal Department of Kansas, had a mere four thousand troops at his
disposal to face an advancing Rebel army at least three times
that size. Kansas Governor Thomas Carney said he doubted that

Kansas was in jeopardy, but rumor ran through the militia that Carney feared that sending the Kansas militia into Missouri could cost him votes in the November election and affect his struggle with Jim Lane for control of the Republican Party in the state. It would not be the first time that opportunism and cynicism lay at the heart of an important military decision.

Both Rosecrans in St. Louis and Curtis in Leavenworth insisted by telegraph that the Kansas militia be mobilized immediately. It was clear as a window pane to all of us in the camp in Lawrence what Price, now short of supplies and needing to arm and equip however many bushwhackers and other locals had joined his invading army, would do. He would take the towns of Lexington and Independence, then capture Westport, south of Kansas City, and, without having to cross the wide Missouri River, swing north to Fort Leavenworth with its huge Federal supply depot, which supported the cavalry regiments that patrolled the plains. And so, on October ninth the Kansas militia *was* called out and on the next day, Curtis declared martial law.

On Wednesday, October twelfth, at dawn a thousand militiamen assembled in Lawrence—as well as hundreds of others in Leavenworth and Shawnee—and by Saturday fifteen thousand men had reported for duty. Curtis stationed the state forces at Shawnee and along Turkey Creek. "Well, we finally get to see some fighting," Jeremiah Whitman said, looking younger than his sixteen years, the few hairs on his upper lip a failed attempt at a mustache. I thought of my son, Henley, two years old on the thirteenth, and wondered if I would ever see my little boy again. "Well, I sure want to see some fighting," Jeremiah repeated, even more bellicose this time. "Tired of all this drilling. Sarge been working me like a rented mule." All the boys laughed and agreed.

Despite the deadly business we were about to undertake, a giddy holiday mood prevailed in our camp. After our latrines were dug and meat was unloaded from the supply wagons, the younger soldiers sported like colts that run and jump in pasture, poke one another with their hooves and whicker. All the boys from Lawrence were here: Punky Paddock, Jeremiah,

Squirrel Searcy, Beedy Biederman, Wheelwright, McDonald, Scott, and others. I watched them knowing that in a few days some of these boys and farmers and shopkeepers would be dead and others would have lost limbs or eyes. Since I had seen men die in John Brown's skirmishes with the Border Ruffians, carried the bleeding to hospital or the mortuary on Black Friday—myself so covered in their blood that when the day was done, like Lady Macbeth, I could not wash the stain from my hands—I could not deny them a last chance to cavort, eat and drink, play cards, listen to a fiddler, or argue about politics.

In the evening a story swept through camp that "Bloody Bill" Anderson, perhaps the cruelest of the bushwhackers had been killed by Union troops in central Missouri; he was reputed to carry with him a silken cord with fifty-three knots, one for every man he had killed, the first fifteen, it was said, from the Lawrence Massacre. I am not ashamed to say vengeance still burned in my heart, and I regretted not being the one to put the final bullet in his head.

After we had eaten our supper, I sat with Dan Cornish, whom I had first met in '56, and now a captain in our militia company. Henry had called him "Danny Boy," but since he was ten years my senior, I called him "Dan." Cornish was a prominent cattle agent and rancher, one of the original Emigrant Aid Society settlers from the days when Sonnet was smuggling Sharps rifles under the noses of the Border Ruffians. A member of the "moderate," anti-Lane faction of the Republican Party in Kansas, he supported Governor Carney and was thought to be a possible candidate for elected office in the future.

Later that evening I wiped down my rifle, for each of us had been issued a new Enfield rifle, although we had hoped for the Henry Repeating Rifles that the Federal cavalry carried. I felt no regret that the promised blue infantry coats and pants had never arrived; we had drilled in our everyday clothes and could fight in them as well. I sat by my campfire's warmth in the cold starless night, trying to write to Hannah—telling her once more of my love—but the young soldiers came one after another to squat beside me for a word or two, although each said he came only for the warmth of my fire. They announced their eagerness for battle, but I could tell they all were scared. I was scared too, although I lied and said there was nothing to fear, hiding my shivers and wondering about the days to come.

CHAPTER EIGHTEEN

The notes of the bugler jerked us awake in a dank half-light, the temperate weather we had left four days before in Lawrence, thirty-five miles away, replaced by gray skies that announced the inexorable slide into an early winter. Most of the company walked lead-footed and weary to the commissary wagon for a breakfast of greasy bacon, hardtack, and black coffee, with the blankets in which we had slept hung around our shoulders. Stopping by the barrel where we filled our canteens, I threw icy water on my face and went in search of Captain Dan Cornish.

"When do we move out, Dan?" I inquired, coming up behind my friend.

"Should know soon, Ezra," he replied curtly. "Depends on Price."

"Our men are jumpy as a pail full of hop-toads," I said. "They say they want some fighting."

"Governor Carney won't let the militia go very far into Missouri. They are . . . after all . . . here to protect the state of Kansas." I thought he said that like a politician clarifying a position.

"And I expect Carney wants them home by November eighth to vote and help keep his faction in power," I opined. He eyed me and then nodded.

"Can't get used to you with a beard," he said, chewing on the piece of hardtack in his hand, "though that cat fuzz on your cheeks don't look like a proper beard."

"Good enough to fight in," I replied with a laugh. "Won't shave 'til I get home again."

"You got tents?" he asked, and I replied with a grunt and a mock shiver.

"Dammit! Supposed to be here yesterday," he cried out, his New England accent so unlike the nasal drawl of most Kansans. Listening to him reminded me of my student days in Boston.

"Curtis is going to trap the Rebs, isn't he?" I asked, although it wasn't a question. "Curtis" was Major General Samuel R. Curtis, commander of the District of Kansas, in charge of all the Federal troops in Missouri and Kansas, the victor of the Battle of Pea Ridge, a crusty, experienced fighter.

"You a Secesh spy then?" He chuckled and pulled at his blue Union jacket to straighten it. "Well, yes, that's what we intend to do. General Rosecrans is following Price's army across Missouri, just south of the river and still heading west toward us. With the Kansas State Militia and General Blunt's cavalry, we'll have him between us. Rosecrans will be the hammer and Blunt—along with *our* militia regiments—the anvil." He pounded his fist into his outstretched palm with a thudding noise.

"Where does the trap close?" I inquired but then continued since I was certain of the answer I would receive. "Somewhere in the hilly, wooded country near Kansas City, where Price's cavalry can't fight as well as on the open prairie, I'd guess. Price will be trying to cross into Kansas to get to Fort Leavenworth, but we won't let him get north. Am I correct?"

"That's the plan—stop him before he gets into Kansas and destroy his army," Captain Cornish said, lowering his voice. "Squash him like a bug!"

"So, we wait for him to come to us," I muttered.

"Only one problem," Cornish said, a concerned look on his countenance. "Governor Carney don't want the Kansas militia to go very far into Missouri. Yes, we wait until Price opens the gate and walks inside. I guess we hit him hard around Independence, *if* nothing goes wrong." Cornish pulled a cigar out of his pocket. "You going to write this campaign up for your paper, Ezra?"

"Yes, plan to. If you remind me of the organization of our army—so I get details right," I replied. I had my diary in the pocket of my buckskin jacket and pulled it out along with a sharpened pencil.

"You probably know this already." We walked to a stone fence and stood beside it. "Of course, Curtis commands the Army of the Border and James Blunt heads his provisional cavalry division," he said.

"I know Blunt from his postings in Kansas." Indeed, I knew Blunt well, a dark, stocky man with a bushy mustache, aggressive, ill-tempered, and coarse, but a fighter. "The sort of man you'd want with you in a barroom brawl," I added.

"Blunt's first brigade is commanded by Doc Jennison; he's Fifteenth Kansas Cavalry now," Cornish continued. "The old Jayhawker. You'd want him in that brawl with you too, even though he's a sonofabitch." Cornish nodded, smiling at his description of Jennison.

"Yeah, know him too. I wrote about him when he commanded the Seventh Kansas—Jennison's Mounted Jayhawkers—when they were lawless ruffians," I said.

"One of the finest cavalry outfits in the Union army now and since the Seventh is part of Rosecrans' army, we may see them here." Cornish paused to see if I were still writing. I nodded at him to continue. "Then there's the Second Brigade under Thomas Moonlight, the tenacious little Scot. Brave and clever. Farmed in Leavenworth before the war started. He *loves* to fight."

"And the Third Brigade of Blunt's division is led by our Colonel Blair—fifteen thousand Kansas militiamen," I said impatiently. "Go on."

"Well, yes, his brigade consists of the Kansas Militia plus the Colored units and the artillery batteries. Except for detachments from Wisconsin and Colorado, the Army of the Border is a Kansas army, Ezra."

"The review helps me, Dan, but you said, '*if* nothing goes wrong.'"

"Listen," Cornish said, walking away from the stone fence against which I stood and then coming back again. "We got about four thousand Federal regulars, Volunteers—the Fifteenth Kansas, the Sixteenth Kansas, the Eleventh Volunteers—and *fifteen thousand* in our *militia*." He spoke, emphasizing the words. "They got no experience fighting. So, I said *if* nothing goes wrong."

"And something *has* gone wrong?" I asked quietly. It was a question I wanted answered.

"On Sunday without General Blunt's knowledge, some of the State Militia were ordered back to Kansas—as you may have heard—the Sixth Regiment. By General Fishback of the Militia Division, who told Colonel Snoddy to take his men home. When Blunt found out, he turned scarlet and cussed out everyone in sight." Cornish laughed but his face was grim. "Took some of his own cavalry, stopped the militia, and arrested Fishback and Snoddy. Militia officer who saw it said he cussed them up and down before he had them led away under guard and then, by God, marched the militia back himself and the militia cheered him along the way."

"How do we fight the Secesh when the militia officers won't take orders from the Union army?" I asked, feeling alarmed by the incident, despite its comic side. "Everybody's counting on us—untrained, untested, raw boys and school teachers and farmers, shopkeepers, workmen who've only shot rabbits and the occasional deer." I had thought of this again and again. Would our militia fight when the Rebel cavalry rode down on them? And, for that matter, would *I* stand and fight? Would I shoot back, or would I run with the boys?

"Just like back home," said Larby Jones, Leona Sonnet's freight driver, now in the militia, walking up to us. He touched the brim of his hat and nodded to the captain, who smiled and stroked his neat black beard.

"'Cept we weren't all carrying guns back home, Larby," Captain Cornish said, slapping me on the shoulder and sauntering away down the road, as I closed my diary. "Gotta go, boys." I found Dan's reference to us as "boys" amusing since Larby was no more a "boy" than I. Just a way for Cornish to remind us of his rank, I supposed.

"Learned one thing about the army, Ezra," Larby announced as several of our Lawrence friends walked up, returning from breakfast with tin cups in their hands.

"Like to froze last night," complained young Biederman, who was listening to us. "That's what I learned." He was chubby and looked younger than most of the boys.

"Lot of what we do seems to be waiting. March in from Law-rence like we're going to battle, then wait," Larby said as the young men strolled off.

"Then wait more," I added, and he laughed, pulling out his corncob pipe and tobacco pouch. "Guess we're waiting now for Rosecrans to chase Price our way."

"Guess so," Larby said, lighting his pipe. "Heard it said war's equal parts boredom and panic. All I know there's going to be a helluva fight when Price gets here."

As though in response to Larby's pronouncement, the pierc-ing call of assembly blew in the distance and another trumpet answered, like two brass-throated birds calling to each other, and all around me our militia was in motion, men rolling up their blankets, putting personal items in their haversacks, and grabbing their rifles. Our band of shop-keepers, workmen, and farm boys formed into their units as we had practiced. The Color Sergeant and the men from the supply wagons lined up too and Captain Cornish soon appeared on horseback—a handsome bay he had ridden from Lawrence—shouting orders and cursing. In the low rumble, voices were briefly distinct before fading into the continuous drone: *moving out, bring on the Secesh, get me a Reb, let's go, dammit.*

Now we saw why we had drilled, as the men moved in an or-derly manner and in step to the drum beat. Some stood waiting for a command while others moved forward away from the grounds on which we had bivouacked. The rattle of bayonets and swords in scabbards, the clang of guns behind the caissons, and thump of ammunition boxes loaded into the limbers ob-scured the separate voices as we marched toward Westport. The Negroes who followed our militia and served as cooks and laun-dresses—men, women, and children—gathered their belongings and straggled behind us, a few pulling small wagons with sad bundles, blankets, and old rugs.

About an hour later, we reached the little hamlet where the Santa Fe and California trails began and marched past the Har-ris House Hotel, where Hannah and I had stopped on our wedding trip, now a Federal headquarters, with officers coming and going or standing in the street. Although a raw breeze had come up, we welcomed the chance to stop and drink from our canteens. I was amazed at the changes since my last visit. Yes, the Indians, trappers, and fur-traders still sauntered down Main Street to the outfitting houses as before, but now blue-coated Union veterans filled the streets, many in formation. Westport had always been a town of divided loyalty, the majority of the inhabitants likely proslavery. Except for our American flag and guidon, our militia could have been Secessionist bushwhackers, since—except for the officers—we were not dressed in Union blue but in the manner of the farm or prairie: buckskin or wool jackets, overcoats, and broad-brimmed hats. When our flag went by, some local boys darted from the alley to throw rocks at us.

We marched east in a gray afternoon, the men singing *John Brown's Body* as we advanced toward Independence—ten miles east of Kansas City—and the Big Blue River, which flowed midway between the two towns. Before dark, the militia reached the bank of the Big Blue and set up our encampment. Taking charge was the quartermaster, Eli Foster, who held the rank of second lieutenant; he had worked side by side with me on the burial detail after Quantrill's raid and was my friend. The men lined up for supper, hungry after the march.

"What news, Eli? I inquired, taking a piece of pork and hard bread from the wagon and joining him at the fire, where other men had gathered. As an officer, he wore a blue Union jacket.

"Takes a while for news to work its way down to me, but I've heard Blunt and Moonlight fought Price in Lexington today," he said, pouring coffee in my tin cup from a big pot. "Tonight, Blunt has retreated to the Little Blue near Independence while Curtis is fortifying the Big Blue—abattis in the fords, gun pits, barricades . . . to wait for the cavalry brigades from Rosecrans' army. They should even the odds."

"Anything else?" I asked, always eager for another detail or two.

"Well, I heard Blunt wanted to fortify the Little Blue, but Curtis ordered him back here. Our militia won't go any farther from the state line. Orders from Governor Carney. Suppose Blunt's hopping mad," he laughed and leaned over to whisper. "Usually is."

I was still chuckling when Eli bid me good night. I wrapped myself in my blanket next to Larby. He was bundled up by the fire and snoring, but not loudly enough to keep me awake.

On Thursday morning the noise in camp woke me before sunup. Eager to warm myself after my morning ablutions, I followed cooking odors to a fire that burned near the commissary wagon. Horse dung steamed in the cold morning air. Limbers with Parrott guns went by, just arriving in camp.

Seeing Negroes in uniform eating bacon and cornbread near the fire, I wondered if they had information about the First Kansas Colored Infantry, the famed Lawrence Volunteer Regiment, who had been victims of a massacre after an April battle near Poison Springs, Arkansas. "You fellows know anyone in the other Colored regiments," I asked. "Got friends in First Kansas. Fought at Poison Springs." I was, of course, wondering what had happened to Alexander the barber and Tiny Tom Pinckney, the huge blacksmith, fearing the worst since no one in town had heard from them for months.

The three infantrymen looked at one another and shook their heads. "Don't know any of the survivors," one said sourly. "But we take no Secesh prisoners now. Bayonet them if they try to surrender. Don't take no shit from them."

"No mercy," the biggest of the three said. "We don't *never* forget Poison Springs."

"Can't blame you," I answered. "It was a cowardly thing to do, dammit." They walked away, leaving me to remember Alexander's pride in his uniform, angry that the Negro Volunteers had been shown no quarter. When after a severe cold spell, as a thaw begins, a huge chunk of unseen ice remains below the surface in the horse trough, so rage for the innocent dead of Lawrence and my friend Henry lay deep within me, made heavier hearing of the slaughter of the Negro infantry volunteers. I wished I could free myself from the painful weight of the past.

It was now full daylight and I could see the Big Blue several hundred yards from us across open ground. Many trees had been felled for the abattis, and I could view our line stretching back toward the Independence Road, down which we had traveled before turning to follow the west bank of the river. Behind us on the higher ground stood oak trees, red-brown penitents dropping their leaves like tears of remorse. Here and there among the oaks, the scarlet of sumac added cheerful spots of color to the gray morning.

The camp buzzed with rumors of heavy fighting on the Little Blue yesterday and the name on everyone's lips was "Moonlight," the little Scotsman. After several hours working on rifle pits and the log barricades above the river, I saw Captain Cornish on horseback, looking melancholy. Knowing I had questions for him, he leaned down from his splendid bay horse and said in a low voice, "No time to talk now. We're still outnumbered on the Little Blue, but Moonlight's Eleventh Cavalry has four howitzers positioned to cover Blunt's retreat. And we think Pleasonton's blue coats are on their way." He turned his horse and trotted south along the river. Major General Alfred Pleasonton was the cavalry commander of Rosecrans' Army of the Department of Missouri and former commander of cavalry in the Army of the Potomac before he opposed plans within the Lincoln administration and was exiled to Missouri. I wondered if he had caught up with the Rebel army, which now should be as close as Independence and moving toward us.

That night many members of our company—especially the Lawrence boys—grumbled as they ate their meal around one of the campfires that flickered and glowed along the banks of the Big Blue, while others waited in silence for the battle which would test all of us. Fiddle music from upriver increased the melancholy of the chill evening.

Although everyone knew the Confederates could not survive another year, it angered me that Price would invade the state of my birth and cost so many lives on the fool's errand of crossing Missouri to attempt to loot Fort Leavenworth. The boys who huddled around the fire might all be dead before the week was over, hundreds of horses killed, and farmland and buildings ruined. What kept Price and his invaders going?

As the first streaks of light appeared in the east, the bugler announced the morning with the clarity of crowing chanticleer. Our pickets were visible against the river, which reflected the pale sky: it was a bright day, but the winter sun provided no warmth. Now we could hear the artillery from the direction of the Little Blue and Independence, and the rumbling of the guns continued throughout the day. By nightfall Friday, word reached us that the superior numbers of the Confederate cavalry had forced Blunt and Moonlight, after taking casualties, to evacuate Independence and retreat, joining us at the Union defensive line on the Big Blue. The Rebels had made several feints, but Curtis would not be drawn into an attack across the river. A storm with sleet and snow had blown in late in the day, and after a meager supper, the Kansans built fires and huddled around them, except for the unlucky pickets who guarded the crossings. I shivered in the cold, thinking of home and my family, and put my overcoat on over my jacket.

Saturday morning was windy and cold, the brilliant sun again affording no warmth. Patches of snow lay unmelted on the ground. I looked for Dan Cornish as I did every morning and saw by his somber face that yesterday's battle had not gone well. Today was the fourth day of skirmishing and probing for weaknesses and we had not forced the Rebels into a fatal error. "Curtis and the generals think Price will try to send his cavalry across the Big Blue, try to outflank us, and get his wagon train into Kansas at Little Santa Fe. He's going south toward Arkansas now—not north towards Leavenworth—and he's got to do it before Pleasonton's cavalry catches up with him."

"Wait a minute, Dan!" I cried, grabbing his arm. "What wagon train?"

"Our scouts tell us Price has three thousand beef cattle and six hundred wagons—loot from his raids across Missouri, protects it like his mother's best silver," my interlocutor explained, a smile briefly crossing his face. "That damn wagon train can go down the Hickman Mills Road and straight to Little Santa Fe unless we cut it off and capture it."

"Then let's hope Pleasonton gets his cavalry here," I interjected. "We're still short-handed, aren't we?"

"Not if all the Kansas militia gets into the fight," Captain Cornish replied. "Have another biscuit, Ezra. You won't get another chance to eat today." He went away laughing.

I was packing my haversack when Eli Foster came up. "Pass the word, Ezra. Our militia looks a lot like the Rebels, no uniforms on either side. So General Curtis wants us to wear a red kerchief . . . or if you haven't got any red, put a sprig of sumac in your hatband," he yelled at the men who surrounded him. "Get going all of you! Sumac!"

"Sumac?" several men standing nearby asked, as I looked for the nearest scarlet-leafed bush, thinking of Malcolm's army in *Macbeth,* each soldier bearing a bough from Birnam Wood as they marched toward Dunsinane. I chuckled as I cut my small branch and carried several to my comrades.

General Curtis's fortifications indicated his belief that the Confederates would attack on the main ford across the Big Blue. All morning desultory rifle fire from across the river kept us behind our barricades, waiting for the attack. Shot rattled through the blackjack saplings behind us or thudded into the logs over which we fired at the flashes or puffs of smoke on the opposite bank. I shot at everything that moved across the river, remembering that John Brown had advised that one should always aim low. Some in the militia complained about the cartridges for the new Enfields, but they seemed to work. Then one of our men was hit and carried to the rear.

Suddenly the wait was over: the Confederate attack had come upstream at Hinkle's Ford near Hickman Mills and by afternoon Rebel cavalry seemed to be pouring across the river below us at Byram's Ford, having turned our right wing. "We been outflanked," I heard an officer yell. "Gotta move now." And we did.

Our supply wagons and artillery rolled up the trails through the woods behind us while our company moved in formation out onto the prairie away from the river, prepared to fight if the Rebel cavalry tried to cut off our retreat. Captain Cornish and two sergeants on foot hurried us along. Several mule-drawn limbers pulling Parrott guns bounced across the prairie and up the hill. The right wing of our line seemed to have collapsed, but most companies were able to retreat in good order. Artillery continued to rumble in the distance and sporadic small arms fire and shouts seemed to come from several directions. The Kansas State Militia—at least what we could see of it—was withdrawing across country followed by our camp followers, fleeing in terror. In an hour or so, cold and exhausted, we reached entrenchments south of Kansas City, and when our lines were established in late afternoon, we heard that the cavalry units commanded by Jennison and Moonlight had retired nearby.

But not all the militia regiments *had* retired in good order, as we learned that night. The Second Kansas Militia from Topeka, who were protecting Byram's Ford, where in the afternoon the Confederates stormed across the Big Blue, were encircled at Mockbee farm after heavy fighting. The untrained farmers and beardless boys fought valiantly against superior numbers of veteran Southern cavalry, losing many men in hand-to-hand combat. About one hundred members of the militia were killed, the same number taken prisoner, many horses were lost, and a brass cannon was captured. It was a grim evening.

As I sat by the fire with Dan Cornish, eating hardtack and bacon and drinking from his flask of brandy, I learned that the Confederates had forced Curtis's entire right flank northward toward Westport, and the Union general had then ordered his left wing to swing or pivot his line back toward Kansas City so that the Army of the Border now faced south instead of east, with picket lines set up outside Westport.

Since Pleasonton was now in control of Independence, Cornish thought Curtis would attack the Rebels the next day on the high and hilly ground above Brush Creek, a shallow stream that runs into the Big Blue, and force Price back into the advancing Pleasonton. Our defensive line, now almost four miles long, ran east and west from the Harrisonville Road to the State Line Military Road. I thought about Curtis and whether the Army of the Border still believed in him. The militia had apparently fought hard, but a regiment or two had been routed. Would Rosecrans and Pleasonton make a difference, and could Price still be trapped between the two Union armies? After four days of preparation and anxiety, the time had arrived.

As I rolled up in my blanket, in the woods just north of Westport, I knew my Company had been fortunate to escape today's losses. My feet were cold and sore, and I was downcast. Death seemed closer than ever for me and my comrades, who slept uneasily with their own fears. My thoughts were drawn to Hannah, whom I saw in my thoughts walking toward me, her body moving slowly in her shift, and I trembled with erotic sensations which almost overpowered me. Would I again kiss her lips or feel her flesh yield to my touch? She seemed a spirit who had come to bid me farewell.

CHAPTER NINETEEN

By four o'clock on a boreal morning, we were in formation, stamping our feet to keep them warm and waiting for orders. The sky was black and moonless, and the cold seemed to rise from the frost-covered ground and seep into our clothing. Our Negro cooks had prepared coffee to accompany the dried meat and hardtack, which usually contained fat grubs, but anything was eatable if one were hungry enough. "Think I'd much prefer weevils to grubs today," Punky Paddock announced in a posh accent, but his jest received no response from a cold and huddled audience. I put a piece of dried meat in my wallet and, when filling my canteen, noted a thin crust of ice on the water barrel. One of the sergeants—Red Sorley—shouted that we were to march through the woods south of Westport to the banks of the stream called Brush Creek, two miles away.

Eli Foster came by, walking his horse. The infantry officers—even second lieutenants like Eli—had their own horses and rode into combat, although they fought on foot. "Just talked to the Captain," he said, and I knew he meant our friend Dan Cornish. "He's superstitious, Ezra. Asked me to promise I'd get his bay horse home to Lawrence if he gets killed today. His sword too." There was agitation in his eyes, so I nodded and answered with a grunt. "He asks you to fulfill this obligation if *I* get killed." He gave a hollow laugh and I nodded again. I took my Colt revolver from my haversack and put it in my waistband under my overcoat. Our Enfields were new, but they were old-fashioned weapons and slow to reload, and a revolver might be useful in close quarters.

"What if I get killed then?" I asked, looking back at him.

"Oh, you can't!" he said. "You got to tell our story so folks will remember us." This was, of course, exactly what I intended to do if I lived. The men in formation with us were all ears—like curious children. "We're going to Brush Creek as soon as more militia regiments come up. We'll be on the right wing, next to Jennison's First Brigade. Moonlight will be on the military road to keep the Secesh from swinging round us and heading for Leavenworth."

"Curtis is determined not to get outflanked again," I opined, listening to Jennison's Brigade, which had bivouacked near us, moving down the hill, horses snorting and neighing, the spurs of the troopers jingling in the darkness.

"The generals were up most of the night at the Harris House Hotel, I heard," Eli replied, almost in a whisper since it was not a suitable time for discourse. Captain Cornish rode by with Colonel Jennison and other officers whom I did not know, Jennison looking like a grizzled dwarf, sitting erect in his saddle and grinding his teeth. I touched my hat brim in salute and Cornish, ramrod straight in his blue coat, acknowledged me with a half-smile.

Now the drummer began his beat and the militia regiment marched off behind our guidon. Red Sorley called out to set the rhythm, with occasional profanities right on the beat. The light artillery batteries creaked behind us as we made our way downhill through the woods, the sound of iron striking iron ringing out in the darkness. Sorley's bushy red beard caught glimmers of light from lanterns carried by the gunners, some of whom rode on the limbers. The pungent odor of horse dung was replaced by the sweet smell of the wet woods as we moved forward in the dark, now depending on noses, ears, and the feel of our feet.

"Keep in line, you asses," Sorley shouted. Somewhere down the hill in the dark on the other side of the creek were the Rebels. I reckoned we would be near Jennison in the center of the Federal line at Wornall's lane, the road up the escarpment onto the prairie, the same prairie across which we fled in our retreat from the Big Blue. The task of the militia would be to fight our way through the woods and push the Rebels back so the cavalry could get to open prairie. Our cavalry was greatly outnumbered, of course: four thousand Union troopers to approximately twelve thousand Rebels—the figures I had written in my diary made it three full Confederate divisions comprising nine brigades. This battle would prove the valor and determination of the militia. I said a silent prayer: let Pleasonton's cavalry arrive in time. Then I whispered to the Lawrence boys who were nearby, took the daguerreotype of Hannah from my pocket, kissed it, and put it back. Off we went at a trot, carrying rifles with fixed bayonets, stirring up the fog which hugged the ground, but at the bottom of the hill we stopped and again waited in the dark.

General Blunt began the attack at daybreak with Jennison's Brigade, led by the Fifteenth Kansas Cavalry, a battalion of the Third Wisconsin Cavalry, and four mountain howitzers. The woods were full of milling and impatient militia. I was not afraid of dying a clean death, but what frightened me was being trampled in a cavalry charge or being shot in the bowels because such a wound resulted in a painful and lingering death. The ambulance crews, I had heard, carried those wounded in a limb to the hospital, but usually left to die those shot in the bowels.

Sergeant Sorley came through the lines to tell us that other militia units were still trying to deploy; some had bivouacked as far away as Kansas City and had only now marched through Westport. The rattle of rifle fire and rumble of cannons came down to us in the woods but still, we did not move. Two hours passed and then we heard our artillery withdrawing down the lane and saw the cavalry retreating to our side of Brush Creek. Sorley was fuming and cursing, and my mood continued to sour. As the Volunteers refilled their cartridge boxes and canteens, word passed along the line that General Curtis had himself come down from the Harris House Hotel to lead the next charge, and within minutes the First and Fourth Divisions crossed the creek, leaving the militia regiments waiting— "like a bride at the altar," the man next to me joked. I was sweating in my buckskins and overcoat. Curtis was no more successful than Blunt, however, and the Union forces were again forced back down the steep hill. Our fortunes were looking grimmer as the morning wore on.

Suddenly Captain Cornish pushed through the militia, our number increasing as more armed men in working-day clothes arrived. A German farmer, it seemed, had informed General

Curtis of a gulch up the hill. Cornish shouted: "We can get behind the Secesh. Follow me! Run! Run!" All of us splashed
across the icy creek as my fear faded away.

Stumbling over rocks and brush, I ran up the gulch with my
fellows behind the guns of the Ninth Wisconsin Battery, which
unlimbered as we emerged onto the prairie. Immediately unlimbered, the battery began firing, tearing at the Rebels' line with
exploding canisters.

More militia, yelling as they ran, followed us up the gulch and
out of the trees. In the distance on both sides, I could see our
line of infantry thick on the ground as windfall apples after a
gale, now striding with rifles behind our star-spangled flag and
the company guidons. To my left, Blunt's mountain howitzers,
which had been crawling up Wornall's lane, roared to life like
hungry lions and, as the Confederate line collapsed, the First
Brigade—in their blue uniforms, bugles blaring, men shouting—
crested the hill above Brush Creek and raced forward to the
stone fences that lined the fields. Horses hit by our artillery
limped away with broken legs or fell under their riders. As I reloaded my rifle, a soldier, out of breath, ran to the stone fence
beside me and dropped to his knees.

"More Rebs than you can shake a stick at," my comrade said,
trying to catch his breath. "This ain't done with." And he was
correct. Yes, we were out on the prairie where the rail and stone
fences which separated the fields gave us some cover, but the
Confederates were retreating to regroup. The spatter of gunfire
was sporadic, and I could hear shots hitting the fence. Thick
smoke now hung over the prairie and Rebel cannon, now firing
from a slope a few hundred yards in front of us, was trained on
our advancing line. Shells exploded in the air above us, shower-
ing us with shrapnel, like the fire and brimstone of Hell, and a
cacophony of metallic fragments fell around us.

Some hit me in the back and shoulders, but none seemed to
penetrate my overcoat. Thinking the Confederate battery might
have targeted the stone fence behind which we cowered, I left
my companion and ran for a lone tree under which several militiamen had sought cover. When I had gone about ten yards, a
shell exploded behind me, the stone fence and my comrade

disappeared in a shower of rock, dirt, and pieces of metal, and I was thrown to the ground unhurt. Perhaps this wasn't my day to die.

All the guns in our several batteries now seemed to be returning fire on the Confederate field guns and through the haze, I could see they were pulling back. After some time, our line of militia and blue-coated Union troopers moved forward again as the enemy withdrew. At last with a pause in the artillery duel, I could hear the rumble of other guns to the rear of the Confederates and now I saw a column of cavalry advancing across the prairie, their flags and guidons catching the sunlight.

Our men cheered loudly at the sight of our Union flag, realizing that General Pleasonton had arrived and was now behind the Rebels. The sun was high in the sky, perhaps an hour past midday; the Union buglers sounded the charge and Jennison's First Brigade, led by the Fifteenth Kansas, came racing past us up Wornall's lane brandishing their sabers. Dust and pieces of dried grass rose in the air as the horses galloped up the lane where Price's cavalry met them head to head and horse to horse. On both sides, men fired pistols and swung their sabers, hacking horse and human, while horses screamed in fright and pain, and men and their animals fell to the ground, bloody and broken. Although I could not reload my rifle in the melee, I took out my revolver and shot at every gray uniform I saw. Then pulling my hat down as if it offered protection from the bullets, I ran for another stone fence.

The Rebels had regrouped near the Wornall house—a mansion surrounded by trees and cornfields—and now they threatened to cut off one of our batteries, the shrill yipping of the Rebels filling the air, but our troopers charged again, creating a press of men and animals: the flat sound of bullets hitting flesh, the falsetto screams of the big horses, unhorsed men with saber in hand, militiamen trampled by hooves, cut open by sabers or shot in the face or gut. I had tried to keep my eye out for the boys from home, but they had disappeared in the maelstrom of crying, limping horses and fallen men, arms twisted, legs shattered.

Crouching against the stone fence, now sweating beneath my overcoat and buckskin gaiters, I reloaded my revolver. A Union soldier, shot in the face and bleeding, staggered toward the fence. As I offered him my canteen, I realized that the Confederate army was again in retreat, leaving the lane before the Wornall house littered with bodies of men and horses, blankets, firearms, sabers, and hats. I helped my wounded comrade toward the house, where dazed and injured from both sides were walking or limping, already a field hospital.

After retrieving my rifle, I noticed a sergeant and my friend Eli gathering the militia units to send after the retreating Secesh. "You all right, Ezra?" he asked, out of breath. "Can't stop to bury our dead. Blunt's gone mad. McNeil was supposed to get between the Rebs and the road to Little Santa Fe. Damned if he didn't let them slip through. How do you let hundreds of cattle and wagons just slip through?" He stalked off. Knowing the Union battle plan, I understood Eli's—and Blunt's—outrage. General John McNeil, commanding Pleasonton's Second Cavalry, had been ordered to block the road to Little Santa Fe, intercepting Price's beef herd and loaded supply wagons, throwing the column back on itself, creating chaos, and capturing them all.

For whatever reason, McNeil had failed to arrive and the Union strategy—the hammer and anvil—had been foiled and the chance at one of the greatest Union victories of the war lost. But we *had* won the battle. Price's army, badly crippled, was now trying to cross into Kansas, going south with his captured supplies. Would we pursue him? As if in answer to my question, the bugle sounded and our Regiment was off, lustily singing *John Brown's Body* as we marched—and marched into the evening.

That night we bivouacked near Little Santa Fe on the open prairie, too hungry and exhausted to celebrate our victory at Westport. In fact, the two Union armies were hopelessly entangled and impossible to reorganize in the dark. I was able to find a few of the Lawrence boys and learn about our militia. Jeremiah, Biederman, and Squirrel Searcy were with me near one of the campfires, but Punky Paddock had been killed as had Dan Cornish. Larby Jones had been shot in the leg and taken to the hospital, where the limb would probably be amputated. Despite the victory, it was a terrible day, and no one knew the fate of the other boys. I was distressed by Dan's death.

Around us were blue-coated Union cavalrymen of the disgraced John McNeil's Second Brigade and, to my delight, the Seventh Kansas Cavalry—the once-notorious Jennison's Jayhawkers, with whom I had spent time in '62. Finally, the supply wagons arrived, bringing ammunition and crackers—only crackers.

Hoping to see some of the men I had talked with two years before, I pushed my way through the blue coats of the Seventh Kansas, many stained with blood or the dirt of combat as the men ate crackers and complained and joked. Warming myself near the fire where a large group of the troopers had gathered, telling stories, I heard a familiar voice.

"Bill Cody," I said, for it was the young Pony Express rider and plainsman in a blue private's uniform. "I thought you'd be a general by now or at least a colonel."

He laughed and grabbed me by the shoulders. "Going to be, Ezra," he said with a merry hoot. "But I got drunk in Leavenworth and when I woke up, I was a private in the Seventh Kansas. And here *you* are . . . but why don't you have a uniform?"

"No money to buy uniforms in Kansas," I replied, shaking my head. "So, you got back home at last."

"Been in Tennessee, got called back to St. Louis, and then sent after Price. Fighting at the Big Blue was tough, but I got a couple of Butternuts," he said proudly. "So, I've been gallivanting round Missouri . . . and not in the highest company neither." Then he paused. "Bet you don't know what I know: Hickok's here!"

"What? Jim Hickok here? In the battle today?"

"Ha! Think you know everything, Ezra?" Cody proclaimed, giving me a look of triumph. "Besides, he's called Wild Bill now."

"I know what people call him," I responded, vexed that this loquacious boy thought he had outfaced me. "Where's Hickok now?"

"Don't know exactly," Cody replied. "But today he rode across the battlefield in a Confederate officer's uniform. Killed a fellow spy turned traitor before he rode into our lines."

"You mean he was a spy for our army?" I asked as he was nodding his head. "All right, Billy," I added, using the name he found embarrassing. "That's powerful news. But I got to get some sleep. Let me know if you see Hickok."

"Probably with his old friend Curtis," Cody continued and smiled. I never knew whether Cody cared if people believed him or not—and I sure didn't believe the Hickok story. I shook his hand and left the Jayhawkers as they were spreading out their blankets.

Stopping at the water barrel, I met a young sergeant of perhaps my age in the uniform of the Seventh, his face disfigured by a deep scar which pulled his lips to one side.

"You from the militia?" he asked in a friendly way.

"Ezra Middleton," I replied. *"Out* of the service, an attorney and writer for a paper."

"Your first fight today?"

"Pretty much," I said, drinking from the tin cup chained to the barrel. "But I did get in one with John Brown—only as observer though."

"A name I revere," he said with spirit. "I come from Pottawatomie, where Brown killed those slavery men . . . but I don't blame him. His son was in the Jayhawkers, you know . . . a Captain, he was . . . Company K."

"Spent time in discourse with him on several occasions," I replied. "I knew he'd left the Seventh. A man of sterling character whom I admired . . . like his father." As I spoke my interlocutor drank water awkwardly from the cup, unable to close his lips completely. "When I visited the Seventh before your Regiment went south in '62, I also spent time profitably with Lieutenant Levi Utt, but I read he was wounded in Mississippi or Alabama."

The sergeant broke in as I paused. "You only know part of the story. First of all, he's still in the Seventh Kansas, a major now. Second of all, he had his foot and part of his leg blown off in . . . let's see, yes, a year ago April in Alabama, captured and paroled, and, when his stump healed, got a wooden leg and rejoined the

Regiment. Third of all, got a new name. Know what it is?" I mumbled that I did not, but he was already continuing his explanation. "Old Timber Toes! What do you think about that? Old Timber Toes!"

I exploded in laughter and the story-teller joined me. "Old Timber Toes," I repeated when I could stop myself from laughing. Utt was only about twenty-five, hardly "old," but this paragon of discipline must have seemed stiff and ancient to young recruits, and clearly it was a name affectionately bestowed.

"And fourth of all," the trooper added with a chuckle, "since you might write this up: a member of his family fought in each of our wars—beginning with his great-grand-pappy in the Revolutionary!" He nodded, spun on his heel, and scrambled over the men lying on the ground wrapped in their blankets like slain soldiers newly interred in shallow graves, mere lumps in the earth.

In the dim lantern light, I found my way back to the company guidon and the fire around which the Lawrence boys slept. As I walked past these exhausted men and dying campfires, I tried to examine and order my thoughts. Our men had reacted to battle differently: some were giddy and exuberant, relieved to be alive and whole; others were quiet and introspective, awed by what they had seen; others again were simply stunned into silence. The images of battle had affected me as intensely as the smell of the choking yellow smoke and gun powder which had so deeply penetrated my garments that I wondered if repeated washings could ever cleanse them. My vexation at Cody was brushed away, but I was determined to find Jim Hickok in one of the two Federal armies. Price had crossed into Kansas—if only barely, since the military road to Fort Scott was the border between the two states. I was certain there would be a pursuit and I wondered if we would be part of it.

After the Battle of Agincourt, Shakespeare's King Henry ascribes glory to God for the English victory over the French. For the Battle of Westport—if that is what the scribes of history choose to call it—perhaps Providence did favor those who fought to save the Union and end slavery, but, if so, He must share the glory with thousands of Kansas farm boys and shop-keepers, each with a twig of sumac in his hatband. My intent was to describe the day, but my eyes and hands were too weary, and I put my diary down. And so, thanking God for my preservation, I committed Hannah and my children to His care and fell asleep.

CHAPTER TWENTY

Reveille awakened me from a heavy sleep, my body stiff and sluggish. Eli Foster and our cooks were unloading bacon and hardtack from the supply wagons which had come from Kansas City during the night. After a supper of crackers yesterday, our company—still missing a handful of men—ate heartily. At their campsite nearby, the Seventh Kansas Volunteer Cavalry—the renowned Jayhawkers—were packing haversacks, checking weapons, and refilling their ammunition boxes. I supposed the cavalry divisions from the two Union armies would lead the pursuit of Price, our infantry following to round up any prisoners or stragglers. "To Horse" was sounded and the Jayhawkers and the rest of Pleasonton's Division followed Blunt's Cavalry Division down the military road which marked the state line.

Unlike the previous two days, Monday was overcast, the sun unable to worm its way through the thick and threatening clouds. Our company in the Regiment—composed of men and boys from Lawrence and Douglas County—was now under the command of Captain Homer Potter, transferred from the Second Kansas Militia after its devastating losses at Mockbee Farm on Saturday. A large and accommodating man, Potter seemed embarrassed by the circumstances of his advancement.

"How's our new Captain?" I asked Eli Foster, who was instructing the cooks about the packing of the commissary wagon, in his shirtsleeves in the chill morning air.

"He'll do," Eli responded. "I'm more concerned about where tonight's supper's coming from. Hope the Army knows where we're going, 'cause I sure don't."

"Did you secure Captain Cornish's bay horse?"

"In the remuda. Probably eating better than we are," Eli laughed. Always a good-humored fellow, I thought, even on the grim burial detail after Black Friday. "Red Sorley's still trying to find our missing," he said soberly. "Four altogether . . . two boys from Lawrence."

The bugler's notes called us to formation and Sorley popped up as if summoned by a spell or some other fairy magic, cursing us as we stumbled into line, poking with his rifle any man he thought recalcitrant. Leaving a few smoldering campfires behind, we marched down the military road, not certain whether we were in Missouri or had crossed into Kansas. "Pick it up!" Sorley called out. "Eight hours behind the Secesh." He gave a harsh laugh and spit at the feet of one he thought out of step. "If we don't move faster, cavalry'll have all the glory."

As we started our march, I remembered times when I had ridden across the tall-grass prairie on a summer's day, the heavens stretching limitless and bright, but the land was now desolate, ravaged and burned in the conflicts of bushwhackers and Jayhawkers, year after year, leaving skeletal chimneys, patches of white ash, and weed-filled, empty fields. A feeling of despair seemed to hang over this ruined countryside.

Why, I wondered, was the militia being sent south after Price? The two Union cavalry divisions would intercept his ill-starred army, impeded by his beef herd and wagons long before we could arrive. Then cheers arose from behind me and our men broke ranks and rushed to gather around one of the missing Lawrence boys, Eddie McDonald, even dirtier than the rest of us. Red Sorley stopped the column with a potful of curses.

"Where've you been, Eddie?" I asked, relieved that he had at last appeared. "You unhurt?"

"Yessir," he said, stopping to gain his composure. "Uncle Ezra, Scott . . . met his death manfully at the hands of the Rebels," the young militiaman replied, as though reciting a lesson at school. With his large gray eyes, he looked like a lost boy about to cry in relief at being found. He brushed at his brown hair.

Sorley had come over, looked at all of us and announced: "Good to know he died like a soldier. Take a minute and then find your place." Sorley seemed relieved to have Eddie back or perhaps just to have him properly accounted for.

"A horse ran him down," Eddie mumbled. "Think his back was broke." He again seemed to struggle with thoughts of his friend's death. "Tried to comfort him but he didn't . . . open his eyes. I followed the army and here I am. Hope somebody . . . buried him." He finally smiled as the other boys continued to congratulate him by pounding on his back and shoulders.

After a few minutes we were again moving south, sometimes marching in a column, more often in the worn-down grass beside the road since the cavalry had preceded us and the road looked like plowed ground, with fresh horse dung which we were loath to march through. Then in the afternoon, rain fell, first as a cold drizzle followed by a steady downpour. Long accustomed to ordering my thoughts as I rode or walked, I moved mechanically as one moves in a dream, without volition. And what was I limning in my mind? The futility of war and its wanton loss of life, policies that benefitted those who make defective cartridges or shoddy boots, supply grub-infested meal and rancid bacon, and seemed to send men to die only to enrich the powerful, lolling in comfort and safety.

Now our feet were slipping in mud that gripped us as though it intended to pull us into its depths. My thoughts had become as foul as the way on which we traveled. Our cavalry carried India-rubber capes or ponchos rolled up behind their saddles; the militia had nothing to keep off the icy rain. At dark we stopped and stood in the cold, waiting for the supply wagons which we hoped would come. But our duty should be uppermost, I told myself, in the struggle to end the great evil of slavery and preserve the Union, and my obligation was to expel the Rebel invaders, who were still fleeing southward toward Fort Scott. So why *had* we been sent south? Perhaps General Curtis thought Price was not escaping to Arkansas but was intending to attack the fort—not as rich a target as Leavenworth, of course, but still a source of food and ammunition for a desperate army.

Some militia regiments had been sent home on Monday morning to be mustered out, Eli told me, so the size of the Kansas militia stood at about five thousand or fewer. My guess was that our two cavalry divisions accounted for seventy-five hundred more, altogether about the same size as the battered Confederate force. All of this I surmised as some of us helped Eli raise the few large tents discovered in one of the wagons. Although the tents were not properly vented, fires could be started out of the rain and we would be able to eat hardtack and salted meat undercover. Nevertheless, we still slept in the rain under our sodden overcoats. I reckoned we were near Paola, Kansas, although I was too exhausted to care. That evening our cooks did not sing as they often did. The mood in our camp was sour.

Early on Tuesday morning, we were awakened, not by the call of our buglers, but the distant rumble of artillery. Our cavalry and its batteries apparently had caught the rear-guard of Price's army, slowed down by his wagons and the muddy roads. Perhaps our militia would again get to fight the Confederates. In the dark and continuing rain, we fell into formation in mud ankle-deep in places, and Captain Potter shouted instructions to our Regiment.

"Pleasonton's Cavalry's caught Price between the Marais des Cygnes and Mine Creek! Can't get his heavy wagons and beef herd up the river banks," he yelled. "A scout from Sanborn's Brigade just talked to the generals. Could be our last battle!" We were too tired to cheer—too wet, too cold, too hungry—but we still wanted to fight once more, and I had a personal vendetta against Quantrill that I needed to satisfy. Off we slogged, about five miles until we neared the river. As we approached Mine Creek, we saw dead horses, dead Rebels in the mud, smashed wagons, discarded rifles, and equipment. It seemed to have been a rout, perhaps a bigger Union victory than Westport. We were ordered to search the woods near the river for Southern deserters and capture them, although some of our number promised they would shoot on sight any Rebs they found. Carefully I went through the scrub oak and ash and hackberry with my Enfield, bayonet fixed, and my revolver in its holster under my coat. In some leafless bushes, I discovered two cowering Confederates, unarmed and shivering, their watery eyes big as silver dollars, hands raised.

"Shoot me, if you must," the older said, "but spare my brother . . . please." Watching them for a moment, I thought of

Lawrence and Quantrill and Henry Sonnet, but I knew I would not kill them, these men who had fought for the wrong cause.

"Can you walk?" I asked and they nodded.

"Let's go then," I ordered, motioning with my head, and marched them to a large corral where hundreds of other prisoners waited to be paroled. They huddled shoulder to shoulder like cattle about to enter the abattoir. Squirrel Searcy, the youngest of our company—small and thin as a drummer boy—guarded a Rebel old enough to be his grandpa, who waited in the line of ragged and dirty prisoners. Already disarmed, they would now swear an oath not to take up arms against the Union a second time before being paroled and left to wander home to Arkansas or Texas. I was surprised to find I pitied them.

Hours later, in the darkening afternoon, Captain Potter rode up and we rushed toward him, hundreds of us, to hear him shout from horseback: "The generals have announced this was a great victory for the Union. Five hundred Secesh captured—two of them Generals Marmaduke and Cabell—and a large number killed." We cheered, although I believe the sight of the supply wagons would have provoked louder ejaculations. Since the drizzle continued, Eli had the men raise the canvas again so that fires could be made, using empty ammunition boxes and broken wagon wheels for fuel. Because no provisions had reached us, the mood of the men who crowded near the fires was as black as Vulcan's stithy. Hunger roiled in my gut, but there seemed little hope that victuals would arrive that night.

Again, we were bivouacking on open prairie, away from the muddy roads, and hoping to find Jim Hickok I walked to where I thought the cavalry divisions had camped. I believed many troopers would know Hickok, famous as a crack shot. Since our campaign began, I had heard four or five versions of a story, when Hickok put six bullets within the "O" of a hanging sign in Kansas City . . . or Topeka . . . or Springfield. Because I would be walking through hundreds—perhaps thousands—of Union troops, I got a piece of red cloth to place in my hatband: everyone had become so accustomed to the red marker during the last week that it was almost like a company badge. If Cody's account were true, Hickok might be serving as a scout or dispatch rider for Pleasonton or one of his brigade commanders, so I searched for the field headquarters. On the trampled dead grass, hungry troopers, having corralled their unfed horses, gathered around meager campfires with nothing but discontent to feed on. Fortunately, the drizzle had stopped.

Pleasonton's Provisional Cavalry was spread out across the prairie like a gypsy encampment, and I found that the troopers of General McNeil's Second Brigade were happy to share with me their curses of the quartermasters, the weather, and the Rebels, as well as to lament McNeil's latest ineptitude, a failure to get part of his brigade into position at the Marais des Cygnes. No one, however, knew the whereabouts of Hickok until I stumbled across Brigadier General John Sanborn's Third Brigade where I struck gold.

I stopped a big fellow in a blue uniform with a blond mustache. "Hickok? Sure, I know him. Everyone does. I'll take you to the scouts' tent," he said, speaking while holding an unlit pipe in his teeth. "Wild Bill, you mean." And so, I was led to Jim Hickok, attired in buckskins, standing outside a tent, cool as an alligator.

"Been looking for you, Jim," I said in greeting. Because of my beard and dirty garments, he didn't seem at first to recognize me. Then he whooped with glee and ran over, taking me by the hand in a hearty greeting.

"By darn, Ezra!" he exclaimed. "Seen hogs cleaner than you. You writing about how we whacked old Price?" He slapped his leg and laughed.

"I'm in the Kansas militia," I said, a little apologetically I must admit. "But we never got uniforms."

"Did give you guns, I hope," he said with more laughter.

"I just wish they'd give us rations," I replied. "All of us are hungry." Several other men in ponchos or overcoats watched us, amused.

"Well, I'm a civilian scout for General Sanborn. Worked for him before." Grabbing my elbow, he drew me toward a fire which another scout was tending. Because the sun had now gone down, a lantern had been lighted. He offered me a campstool and sat on another, stretching out his long legs before the fire.

"They didn't bring rations up tonight—or fodder for the horses either." He paused for a moment, then asked: "How's your beautiful gal, Hannah? I need to pay you a visit when this damned war's over."

"I've got two children now—Samantha and Henley. All in good health and safe when I left home."

Hickok suddenly looked grave. "Sorry. Forgot about it—Quantrill's raid. Terrible from what I hear." His voice was low. "Unarmed men slaughtered or burned alive. Work of a coward." He shifted on the stool. "How'd you survive?"

"I was coming back from Kansas City. Missed them by an hour or so—or you wouldn't be talking to me now." My laugh didn't change his solemn face. "So, I joined the militia . . . and I've had a rage inside ever since to pay the Rebels back for Lawrence. More than a year now." We looked each other in the eye, and he nodded.

"Know what you mean," he said, touching his revolvers idly, as one might brush back his hair or scratch his nose.

"Looking for retribution," I added. "Thought I'd get it on this campaign. Hoped we'd find Quantrill with Price." I gave another laugh and Hickok chuckled softly.

"Fellow betrayed me at Westport—Dave Tutt. Got my mate killed. Almost got *me* killed." I nodded to show I knew about betrayal.

"Jim, I saw Cody at Little Santa Fe with the Seventh Kansas." Hickok sat up straight in surprise. "Cody said you were galloping across the battlefield in a Confederate officer's uniform. Rode into our lines with another man!"

"Guess that would be Tutt . . . but I weren't in a Confederate uniform at Westport," Hickok said emphatically.

"Never know what to make of Cody's stories," I said, moving closer to the fire.

"Guess I'll see Tutt down the way," he replied, as calmly as if he were talking about scraping mud off his boots, but I knew what he meant. One day Hickok would meet Tutt face to face in public and both would draw—like a trial by combat in the Middle Ages or a duel in Shakespeare—and the guilty one would die because God always saw to it that justice prevail, or so many people believed. And on the frontier, a man would never be found guilty in court if he killed another man in a fair fight.

We sat for a few minutes quietly and then Jim pointed toward the south where the dark skyline was suddenly bright. "I thought it would come tonight." Then explosion after explosion split the night's silence and aerial bombs spread out in patterns like fireworks on the Fourth. "You see, Price's set his wagons on fire. He couldn't have lasted another day with them. Too slow and cumbersome for these roads and creeks, and now he's out of provisions and can't attack Fort Scott. He's a snake chopped in pieces and those pieces won't grow legs."

"How far *are* we from Fort Scott now?"

"I'd say six or seven miles. We're in Kansas—west of the fort. When Price gets to the Arkansas Border—if he gets there— what's left of his army won't be large enough to constitute a good bodyguard." Hickok gave a melancholy laugh. "Say!" he said, rising from the camp stool. "Found persimmons in the woods today. Just fall from the trees when they get ripe." As he went into his tent, I marveled again at the tall man's catlike grace and amiable disposition and wondered whether he would thrive in a time of peace.

"Many thanks, Jim," I said, taking the dirty kerchief he offered me, filled with a fruit I loathed. "Make a nice little supper." It was time to wend my way back to the militia and, since my clothes were dry, have a sound sleep. "Come see us in Lawrence, Jim," I said, shaking his hand. "Want you to meet my young ones."

"First, I'll send a letter, Ezra . . . to Hannah," he said in jest as I walked away.

As I went back to where I had left our company, the troopers of Pleasonton's Division were bedding down around their campfires. On the horizon, I could still see the glow from the burning Confederate wagon train lighting the moonless dark. The meeting with Hickok left me with a sadness I couldn't name. The war was ending, and changes were coming: the frontier was being transformed by the railroad and telegraph, and farmers were plowing the prairie where herds of bison once roved. Although I knew Hickok to be a man of rectitude, he was violent as well. He loved danger and adventure as other men love women, money, or fame; his talent—a unique talent—was his skill as a gunfighter. Certainly, in times of peace, he could work as a lawman or pursue daring enterprises farther west, but, I feared, someday in a moment of inattention or through inauspicious circumstances someone would kill him. Perhaps he knew this too but also understood he couldn't avoid his fate.

Although I had often thought of writing about Jim Hickok, I knew I would not. Not that I thought I lacked the faculty to record his qualities. Rather, I felt that readers would expect tales of bloodthirsty sensationalism, tales which would be false to the man and would attract hotheads seeking to test their skills or embellish their reputations by confronting him, or, even worse, to rob him of his renown, shoot him from behind. Hickok had no notches in his pistols—the mark of a braggart—and never exhibited vainglory or was given to boasting. To write about him would have been a betrayal of our friendship.

By the end of the evening my desires for revenge had diminished, replaced in my mind by a favorite quotation of my father's, Prospero's speech near the end of *The Tempest*, a speech in which he forgives his enemies:

> *Yet with my noble reason 'gainst my fury*
> *Do I take part. The rarer action is*
> *In virtue than in vengeance.*

I said these lines to myself again and again as I walked, cold and hungry but with my mind now at ease. Soon I passed our pickets and found my way to my blanket and haversack next to Jeremiah Whitman, lay down, and quickly fell asleep. I had put the kerchief of persimmons next to the young soldier.

When I heard reveille blown, I thought I had just fallen asleep. Pleasonton's Cavalry Division had already departed but I had heard nothing. My hunger gnawed like a rat inside me, but Captain Potter had ridden up with Eli, and the whole Company ran to them, thinking they would announce that rations were coming. "We're marching to Fort Scott," Potter announced. "Plenty for us to eat there. The march will sharpen your appetite." Everyone growled at his jest or swore under their breath, but they swallowed their curses when Eli raised his hand and began to speak.

"Here's what I got to say!" Eli shouted. "We need to take Captain Cornish's horse and sword back to his wife. I say we eat today at Fort Scott . . .." A cheer arose from every throat, as loud a cheer as I've ever heard, but Eli still had his hand raised and the men were quiet, waiting for what would come next. "After which we'll be mustered out of service, and then—tomorrow— the "Sumach Millish" will march home. For us, this war is over!"

CHAPTER TWENTY-ONE

Bullets whined over my head like malign, invisible bees which rattled in the dry leaves and slapped into the bodies of men and horses, screams of pain and terror and the sounds of iron being struck like the blows of the blacksmith, the sulfurous smoke of battle thicker than fog suddenly lifting to reveal uniformed bodies strewn fantastically on the ground where death had indifferently scattered them . . . then with a jerk, I awakened. It had been a dream and, sweating and breathing heavily, I struggled to my knees, remembering with relief we were in Fort Scott and that today we would march home.

"Going home, Uncle Ezra," Jeremiah Whitman shouted with more than his usual exuberance as we came out of the barn. Because the total number of our Regiment—less the sick, wounded, dead, or missing from our campaign—stood at more than eight hundred, several of the militia companies had been forced to sleep in the barns, but we felt grateful that for the first time in two weeks we had a roof over our heads.

The Fort Scott Road runs from the fort and town west and north to Lawrence—a more direct route than the military road down which we had come from Little Santa Fe. Going north it crosses Pottawatomie Creek, the Marais Des Cygnes River, and the Santa Fe Road, before reaching Lawrence. In Fort Scott, we had been mustered out of Federal service—twenty-three days total, according to Captain Webster, the mustering officer. And so, on Thursday, October twenty-seventh, we marched out of the fort with flags and guidons flying. Our four ambulances were filled with sick men and boys, suffering from ague or dysentery. Captain Potter had acquired several mule-drawn wagons as well, for recovering militiamen who were still too weak to march.

Silas Saltmarsh, owner of a Lawrence tannery, marched beside me and his wounded brother Paul rode in one of the

ambulances, behind which walked several Negroes hired by
Captain Potter as nurses. Our company followed Potter and Eli
Foster, who rode on horseback, Eli leading Captain Cornish's
handsome horse. "Well, looks like we'll be back by election day,"
Saltmarsh announced, saying the obvious. "Everybody knows
I'm fixing to vote for Old Abe." I could see him watching for my
reaction. Then he spoke again. "Think he'll get a second term,
Ezra?"

"Hard to tell," I responded. "Some folks are angry about the
draft, and some may just like McClellan." Out of the corner of
my eye, I saw Saltmarsh frowning, so I added, "despite McClellan's failure to win any battles."

"Well, the Union occupies Atlanta and all of Tennessee . . .
and Grant's laid siege to Richmond," he said, his voice rising,
perhaps contentiously. "Deserves another term, he does!" And,
of course, I agreed with him but was loath to venture an opinion, not having seen a newspaper in three weeks and knowing
nothing of recent events.

As we marched, I listened but paid little heed to my comrade,
who talked of Republican politics, Captain Cornish and Governor Carey and Jim Lane, for I was still troubled by my dream,
hoping I would not revisit those scenes of battle again in my
sleep. Since I was unresponsive, Silas fell silent and I could
think of Hannah, drawing from my memory a single line from
Twelfth Night: *journeys end in lovers meeting*. That sentiment
comforted me, for in two nights I would be home with Hannah
and my children.

When we stopped for dinner at noon, Eli had the cooks bring
out ham and bread, carrots and apples. Because we had left the
rain behind, we marched on dry roads in the cold, making good
time—Sergeant Red Sorley saw to that—the Regiment stretching
out snake-like behind us. As the column swung further from the
state line and its ravaged landscape, we saw more farmers driving cows toward barns or mending fences before the snows
arrived, and, as they recognized our flags, they cheered us and
waved their hats. By nightfall, we camped at a creek west of
Trading Post to replenish our supply of water. I reckoned we had

come far enough to reach Lawrence by Saturday evening as we intended.

The mood was gay until a Negro who cared for the sick and wounded in the ambulances announced that Beedy Biederman had fallen victim to dysentery or whatever it was that had sickened the Regiment, some of whom had perished. A terrible irony it seemed that a young man unscathed in battle should succumb to disease—and so close to the safety of home. On a piece of an ammunition box Corporal Ellsworth elegantly incised with a bowie knife: *Henry Biederman. Hero at Westport Battle. K.S.M. Died Oct 27, 1864.* Wrapped in canvas, he was placed in a grave which his comrades dug, and Captain Potter read from the Bible and prayed for the soul of the young soldier. I did not remember that his given name was "Henry."

After the burial what remained of the company of Lawrence boys sat by the campfire with hardtack and coffee, talking of Biederman. Of course, I knew that as many soldiers died of sickness and disease as combat wounds, but his loss was a shock which had dampened the humor of the entire company. It was, then, a relief of sorts when Saltmarsh, sat next to me and returned to his praise of Lincoln. "My paper has always supported Lincoln," I replied to him, suggesting that the country now needed the President more to heal the wounds of the nation than to prosecute a war which was almost over. "When the last Southern army had surrendered, we must welcome the Rebels back as brothers who have strayed, rather than enemies . . . but we must protect the rights of the new Negro citizens too."

"Can't the Republican Congress see to that?" Silas asked. I thought I heard a note of challenge in his voice.

"That will take a constitutional amendment," I said. "As you remember, the Emancipation Proclamation freed slaves only in states in rebellion. Slavery must be ended everywhere in the country." I regretted sounding like a pedagogue in a classroom.

"Well, that's right," he asserted, nodding vigorously and gesturing with his pipe. "People forget that. Lincoln's a shrewd politician—can twist arms in Congress, make deals to get votes!" He chuckled and winked at me. "That shit's what Republicans do in Kansas."

"What they do in Washington too, I wager. Still, better than killing people," I asserted, laughing. "But you said it this morning, Silas. Lincoln must be re-elected." Saltmarsh arose and knocked out his pipe, saying he needed to see his brother. Somehow the industrious Eli had secured a wagonload of blankets at the fort and so the Douglas County company slept warmer now, many already wrapped against the cold and damp. Perhaps they were dreaming of home.

Friday morning was cold and windy, but no one stayed long around the breakfast fire so eager were we to continue the trek home. On the road, a Federal supply convoy met us, evidently bound for Fort Scott, strung out like an archipelago of wagons in a sea of rust brown and purple grass. Since we were marching with our Enfields and only our officers wore Union blue uniforms, the drivers shouted questions as we passed them.

"Kansas Militia," one of our men shouted in reply to questions. "Beat the Rebels like a drum at Westport!"

"Then beat 'em again at Mine Creek," added one of the soldiers from Lawrence, laughing, as the teamsters driving the mule wagons hooted and cheered. Captain Potter had stopped to talk to the squad of troopers who rode with the convoy and now trotted back toward the head of our column. Before we stopped for dinner, I recollected that we were near Dutch Henry's Crossing on Pottawatomie Creek, where John Brown had struck out in vengeance against his foes in '56. Gray clouds seemed pasted above the fields and bare trees chattered in the wind, but in places, sunshine broke through.

When we crossed the muddy Marais des Cygnes, crows cawed at us from the treetops before flapping back into the safety of the woods. Here and there farmhouses and shocks of corn like sentinels seemed to announce mile by mile we were approaching home. Hawks floated in the winter sky, searching for rabbits and mice in unharvested fields. As the late afternoon sun slid out of a shelf of clouds, turning them gold and vermillion, we made our fires and ate our supper as the evening chill descended.

We were past Osawatomie, almost to Palmyra. One more night until I will be with my family, I told myself as I prepared my blanket on the ground, glad at last to take off my shoes and rub my sore and blistered feet. The last thing I remember before sleep overcame me was the nickering of the officers' horses in tether.

In the morning, although weary from two days of marching, I readied myself by wrapping my sore and bleeding feet with strips of cotton rags that Eli had given me to replace my tattered socks and washed myself in a basin of cold dirty water.

"How do you fare today?" I asked Squirrel Searcy as we lined up for a breakfast of side pork and bread toasted over the fire. It was Saturday and tonight we would be home.

"Fit as a fiddle," he replied, this quiet boy with little rodent's eyes and protruding teeth. "No rain and no hardtack." Several of the men drinking coffee nearby laughed, Squirrel seeming pleased with their reaction. Everyone was eager to set out and several of the militiamen who were still at the latrine had to run to catch up with the departing column, like calves separated from a herd. The air was cold, nipping at my ears and nose. As I waited for Red Sorley's orders, I hugged myself against the wind.

As we neared the point where the Fort Scott Road crossed the Santa Fe Road as it headed west, wagons and riders met us, giving way to our column, and onlookers ran from houses to shout welcome to us. As the miles fell away and despite my painful feet, I discovered new reservoirs of strength as I thought of Hannah, my children, and home.

Once we reached Brooklyn, Eli planned to ride ahead to deliver his grim message to Maude Cornish and return Dan's horse and his sword, then gallop the remaining three miles to Lawrence, where he would announce that the victorious militia had returned. Because the telegraph line had been extended to Lawrence in the spring, everyone in town already knew the Union armies had expelled the Confederate invaders, but the accounts in the local papers would not have revealed the names of those who died or had been maimed and those who would arrive safely at home.

As I had hoped, the sun had not yet set when the Douglas County company and the pitiful remnants of the Second Militia Regiment from Topeka crossed the California Road at Blanton's

Bridge over the Wakarusa and entered town. A few riders had already met us, cheering as we advanced down Massachusetts Street to the commercial district, our flags flying, the hastily-assembled town band playing martial music. Although my feet hurt so badly that I limped all afternoon, I was determined to march proudly into town with our company, my shoulders back and my head held high. I felt relief mixed with guilt to have returned safe in life and limb, but I could not forget how some had paid with their lives for our victories. Familiar faces smiled and voices I recognized shouted, as I searched for Hannah's face in a crowd assembled three and four deep near the Liberty Pole. Finally, I saw Leona and Isaac Worthy as Captain Potter gave the signal, Red Sorley shouted "Dismissed," and the men rushed to their families.

"Oh, Ezra," Leona sobbed as she pushed through the cheering crowd and took my arm. "Your babies have been ill," she said. "Henley quickly recovered." Now tears flowed down her cheeks as she struggled to speak again. "But Samantha sickened on Wednesday . . . Three days ago. Hannah hasn't left her bedside. Lung fever!"

"Samantha? Will she live?" I asked, hugging our weeping friend and desperately searching her face for an answer to my question. Isaac had brought the buggy around, and I limped toward it.

Taking my Enfield and haversack from me, he said, "Mighty glad you made it home, sir." A line from Shakespeare, sadly appropriate, came into my mind: when King Henry receives news of a great military victory as he lay dying: *Will Fortune never come with* both *hands full?* Must the good so often come knotted with the ill?

"More sad news, Leona. Larby's been hurt and may lose a leg." I said as we climbed into the buggy. "Dan Cornish is dead and three of the Lawrence boys."

Leona gasped before she spoke. "Everyone in town knows of your victory," she answered, her voice strained by sorrow. "All of us have been praying for our Kansas boys. But so much death, so many lost."

As we entered our barnyard, I jumped from the buggy as Isaac reined in the horse and I ran lamely past my dog, Caesar, barking excitedly at my return. In the kitchen I found Hannah, her hair down and eyes red from sleeplessness and weeping, Henley peering timidly from behind her. She ran and held me tightly as I took him in my arms. "It's pertussis—whooping cough, Ezra. An infection of the lungs. Samantha is very ill." They had been attended, she told me through her tears, by Dr. Virgil Gafney, who treated the wounded on Black Friday.

"But are *you* well?" I asked, looking into her eyes.

"Yes, now you are home. I feared you had been killed. I cursed myself for letting you leave . . . even as I knew you had to go." She paused, looking at me. "Is your foot injured?" I answered her question with a shake of my head. "And you have a beard and dirt on your clothes."

"How long has our little girl been ill?" I asked as Leona came into the kitchen. Although our friend had moved to her new house months earlier, she returned when I left with the militia. Hannah was boiling water to put by Samantha's bed, hoping the moisture in the air would have a salubrious effect on her lungs.

"Three days, my dear," Hannah replied, "but still she doesn't improve. Her cough keeps her from sleeping and she is now very weak."

"While you look in at Samantha, I'll fix you a hot supper," Leona said. "And heat more water for a bath." I crept into the children's room and looked down at my daughter's face, the freckles across her cheeks more prominent against her pale skin—and my heart ached. Although I knew that children often died in infancy on the frontier, to say so to my wife would not console her. Over the years almost every household had lost a baby, commonly in winter. Death visited the family hearth as well as the battlefield but knowing this did not lessen the pain. Three young boys from our town did not return to their homes, having passed through the narrow gate of death which one must enter alone. I felt sorrow for the grieving families.

The next day I sat with my daughter in the morning before calling on the parents of the three boys who had died: Henry

Biederman, Punky Paddock, and Edgar Scott. I would ride out to see Maude Cornish when I was able.

Later in the day, I sat with Samantha again, wiping her flushed face as I listened to her wheeze and cough. When she slept, I transcribed from notes my words about the recent campaign against Price. Although there was now a telegraph office in Lawrence, I thought I would send Downing my lengthy account by mail. Since the outcome of the Union victories on the Border was already well known and attention was now being paid to the presidential election and what everyone assumed were the dying days of the collapsing Confederacy, Downing might, in fact, have little use for my descriptions. Samantha's condition continued unchanged, and I wondered if her little lungs could sustain life.

Then on the second day after our return, Samantha's health ameliorated, her breathing became less labored and coughing no longer shook her body. Dr. Gafney, who had visited her every day of her confinement, expressed confidence she would recover. Hannah and Leona smiled and laughed again. I thanked Providence for saving our child and, fearing a relapse, continued to pray for her health. For me, the events of the autumn had yet again been grim instruction in the mutability of life and fortune.

Tuesday, November eighth, was Election Day, traditionally on the frontier a day of patriotism and display mixed with hard drinking. It was cold with the sun winking out from behind clouds of chicken-feather-white which floated across the sky. After casting my vote for Lincoln and the moderate Republican faction of Governor Carney, I sought out Eli Foster, who always knew the whereabouts of whiskey, standing on the board sidewalk across from the polling station; with him were Silas Saltmarsh and his recovering brother Paul, sharing a twist of tobacco and a jug. With them were several of the boys from the militia, no longer regarding themselves as boys but now as men, joking and cursing.

"Well, Uncle Ezra, we sure beat the Rebels all to smash, didn't we?" Jeremiah greeted me, pulling a humorous face, one never loath to stifle a boast.

"I know no more about that than a hog knows about a holiday," I replied, and the men guffawed, Jeremiah joining in.

"Lincoln will be elected," Silas declared, leaning close as he talked so I could smell the whiskey and tobacco on his breath.

"What do the Eastern papers say, Ezra?" Eli asked and everyone watched me, supposing me an authority of some sort, a role with which I have always been uncomfortable.

"In the country there's discontent," I began, "and Lincoln may be blamed by many, but I'm hopeful he'll receive enough electoral votes," I said this because I believed only Lincoln could restore our shattered country—certainly not McClellan.

"Don't change horses in mid-stream!" Paul Saltmarsh said, as plain-spoken as his brother. "Kansas will vote for Abe."

"Maybe not New York City," Eli interrupted. "Draft riots there in '63, and hundreds were killed. That was in the papers."

"We still say Abe will win," Silas said confidently. He rubbed his hands together in the morning chill.

"Well, the telegraph will get the news here by tomorrow," Eli said. "This time tomorrow we'll know."

And Eli was right. By the end of the day on Wednesday, the *Lawrence Journal* and the *Lawrence Daily Kansas Tribune* were reporting an impressive Lincoln victory in the Electoral College, based on what seemed a substantial margin in the popular vote. Eli also proved an astute observer: Lincoln did, in fact, lose the popular vote in New York City, although he won the electoral votes for the state. And I was pleased that Lincoln won the three electoral votes from Kansas.

Despite the cold, that night people gathered near the Liberty Pole and around the newspaper and telegraph offices, and at the hotels and in the saloons, men toasted one another and cheered. Since Samantha was now able to leave her bed, I kept myself away from the celebrations to enjoy home, a comfort even greater than knowing Lincoln would continue to guide the Republic.

When the nation celebrated its second Thanksgiving two weeks later November twenty-fourth, there was much to be grateful for. Although the solid sheet of ice on the horse trough announced the beginning of another iron-hard winter in our state, the sky, although overcast, was bright for the holiday. Leona, who had moved back to her own house when I returned, was driven to our home by her indispensable agent, Isaac. I was surprised when Hannah asked Isaac to join us for dinner; at first, he demurred but, seeing my wife glance at me, I insisted he stay, and he did. I believe it was the first time I had sat down to a meal with a black man, but it was Isaac, with his impeccable manners and intelligent conversation, not me, who put all of us at ease. Our other guests were Eli and the new schoolteacher Prudence Franklin, neither of whom seemed offended to eat with Isaac.

Although General Sherman now occupied Atlanta and General Grant continued to lay siege to Petersburg and Richmond, the progress of the war was not the subject of our social intercourse. What *did* provoke conversation was the Thirteenth Amendment, which would soon be voted on by the House of Representatives, having earlier passed the Senate. Eli asked about the vote in the House, and I responded by relating Russell Downing's opinion in the *Globe Democrat*. Although many newspapers believed the Amendment would fail, Downing opined that Lincoln was a master strategist with an iron will: somehow it will be done, Downing had written. All those at the table concurred.

The blessing being asked, the dinner which followed was a feast worthy of the new holiday: a hen from our flock and ham from our smokehouse, potatoes from the root cellar, cornbread stuffing, and carrots cooked in brown sugar, followed by pies of several kinds. Henley crawled on the floor while Samantha sat at the table beside her mother eating potatoes with her fingers. I thought of family and friends who were no longer with us: chairs were empty at many tables.

When Hannah and Leona had served the final course and the guests seemed ready to leave the table, I said: "Today we again give thanks to God for his many blessings." Hannah smiled at me. "Our child survived a deadly sickness, Lincoln was re-elected, and The War of the Rebellion is soon to end with the Union preserved." All of those gathered together nodded at my words, and Eli thumped the table with his fingers as the others smiled.

Hannah surprised me by speaking. "Had I the foresight of Cassandra I could not say what may lie ahead." She paused for a moment, and then added: "But if I were Cassandra, you would not believe me anyway." There were chuckles and laughter around the table. "I hope it is not amiss for a woman to speak about politics." She did not wait for objections to be raised. "The South is impoverished, many of its cities in ruins and its croplands abandoned, and millions of former slaves without sustenance or direction. So, I know you will agree with me when I say our watchword for today and tomorrow must be—reconciliation. Ezra and I have a great love for Shakespeare. One of our favorite plays is his *King Lear.* When the aged and broken king is reunited with his daughter Cordelia, the daughter he has angrily cast aside, he says simply: 'Forget and forgive.' Despite our grievous personal losses, that is what we must do." I thought what she said was splendid and our guests thought so too.

Now all eyes turned to me as the host. "I don't wish to play the orator. Hannah has spoken with an eloquence I do not possess. But I feel compelled to add this: I saw President Lincoln only once—giving a speech in Elwood on the sad day in '59 when John Brown was hanged in Virginia." My passion rose within me, my mouth went dry, and my eyes seemed about to water. "Lincoln was not a handsome man—tall, a bit awkward perhaps, and sad of countenance—but I saw in his face that day a compassion I have seen in no other human being. I thank Almighty Providence—in a time of crisis—for giving us such a man."

July 4, 1876

Today is the centennial of our independence from Great Brit-
ain—Independence Day—and eleven years since the end of our
Civil War or the War of the Rebellion as some in Kansas still call
it. It is high summer, the sun brilliant, the day hot, and Lawrence a thriving town of businesses and shops, flower gardens,
lawns, and trees. As I sit on the porch of my new two-story brick
house, I remember the raw town I entered twenty years ago in
May of 1856.

As the town prepares for the Independence Day parade,
bands are tuning up in South Park on Massachusetts Street,
where Quantrill's raiders assembled in 1863 before beginning
their despicable acts of murder and arson. Flags are hung on
our major thoroughfares, and red, white, and blue bunting is
prominently displayed on shops and homes. Soon veterans of
our wars will assemble and march down Massachusetts to
cheers and applause. I will not march in today's parade since,
as a Kansas militiaman, I had no uniform, despite my time in
service. Besides, I believe the cheers are owed to the Union Volunteers, who often served for three or four cruel years, marching
again proudly in Union blue, some with a sleeve which once
possessed an arm, flapping as they stride by, and one or two
others with an empty pant leg, limping bravely on crutches.
Those who were officers ride on horses which they may have
bought from the government when they were mustered out. Like
the horses, the men look older than when they served, and some
who had black hair and beards are now bald or gray. Food and
beverages are being unpacked in South Park and fireworks wait
in boxes for the sunset, empty chairs ready for their occupants.
And as I sit in the shade, waiting for Hannah and our children

and remembering the past, there is a face and a name for every story that demanded to be told.

My career as a news correspondent for the *Globe Democrat* is as dead as the men and boys who fell at Westport, and I am now an attorney. Twenty years ago, I arrived in Lawrence, a young man of twenty-two years, having come west to discover grand themes for the novels I intended to write. During those years, I knew men of notoriety and renown, some capable of monstrous evil, others exemplars of heroism and self-sacrifice, and still others ordinary in the eyes of the world but nevertheless with some special talent not to be gainsaid. Their stories and the bloody birth of Kansas amid a decade of violence I have attempted in the foregoing pages to relate.

E. P. M.

ABOUT THE AUTHOR

ALAN ELLIOTT CRAVEN is a retired Shakespeare scholar and former college dean residing with his wife, Janice, in San Antonio, Texas. He has three adult children. Born in Kansas City, Missouri, he lived in Lawrence, Kansas for a number of years. His family has deep Midwestern roots, the Cravens settling in Missouri before 1830. As boys, his father and uncle knew the outlaw Frank James in Kearney, Clay County, Missouri. His mother's family moved to Kansas in 1861, the year the state was admitted to the Union. They homesteaded at Dry Ridge, Bourbon County, Kansas. Nine boys in the family fought for the Union in the Civil War, including his great-grandfather. In the presidential election of 1860, his great-great-grandfather and two other men were the only ones in their precinct to cast votes for Abraham Lincoln.

www.ingramcontent.com/pod-product-compliance
Lightning Source LLC
Chambersburg PA
CBHW032119020726
47494CB00007BA/2145